The Kingdom Child

Endorsements and reviews

Jennifer and Rosalyn,

This is my first attempt at trying to put into words a few thoughts that I hope will encourage those reading them to take the next step and read *The Kingdom Child*.

In early March of 2011, I had the privilege of meeting an extraordinary young man and his amazing family. The call came to my office explaining that a thirteen-year-old boy had asked to be baptized the following Sunday, and I just happened to be the pastor scheduled to do baptisms that morning. This request came with some challenges. Jordan Allen was confined to a wheelchair and would have to be carried up two flights of stairs to our baptistery and back down. In addition, we would need assistance to carry him down into the water, as well as back out after baptism. It was a rally cry to help this young believer in Jesus Christ overcome his physical obstacles in order to fulfill a deep desire to follow Christ in believer's baptism. Two young men in our church volunteered to help make it happen. And so it did, on March 13th. If there was a dry eye in our 2,000-seat worship center after his baptism, I didn't know about it! This was a moment in time I will recall with joy and great emotion the rest of my days.

It was barely a year later that I received another call; on a rainy weekday morning, as the streets around us were flooding during an outright and relentless downpour. This message required an immediate response. I left the building, waded in knee-deep water to my car, and raced toward the Methodist Hospital in Sugar Land, Texas to meet with Jordan's family. His heroically-fought battle with brain cancer had come to an end.

The Kingdom Child is about this wonderful young man. It's also about his unconditionally loving family. Love, hope, and faith describe their often-agonizing journey through what we'd all probably agree is life at its toughest. Jordan's faith wrote this book, really. Jennifer Johnson captured the vision and put it down on paper. Jordon inspired her to tell his story in such a way as to give us a glimpse of what is and what it could be for people who live life with their hearts wide open to God's promises, even in life's most heart-wrenching circumstances.

The Kingdom Child Testimonial
by John Rushing, Pastor of Adult Ministries
Sugar Creek Baptist Church, Sugar Land, Texas
www.sugarcreek.net

***

Jennifer, I know you were led by the Spirit because I could clearly picture in my mind what your words described, and the visions given to me were amazing. These visions were amplified by recently seeing the movie, *Miracles from Heaven*, especially when the young girl's out of body experience reminds her of the Monet painting she saw in the museum. I also loved the end of the book and the perfect arrangement of the Scriptures.

Jennifer Johnson, a powerful witness of the transformative power of God's love in her own life, has written an emotionally-draining, heart-wrenching, touching story, *The Kingdom Child*, of a family's faith journey as it has to deal with the unexpected, tragic loss of their teenage son. This book will definitely encourage you to carefully examine the foundations of your Christian faith, to make sure it is built on a firm foundation that will not be shaken when the storms of life come, and to encourage you to surrender completely to the Spirit, so the Spirit can conform you to the Image of God's Son, so God's Kingdom purposes can be achieved through you on earth as it is in heaven, so that your light will shine before men that they may see your good works and glorify your Father which is in heaven!

Blessings to you and our family
Jennifer.

— Edgar H. Case

***

I loved this book! I couldn't stop reading to find out what would happen next. Although I found the strong faith in the will of God held by Jordan's mother to be unbelievable, I completely accepted Jordan's account of encountering Jesus. It described God and the afterlife as realistically as could be imagined, and touched an elusive sense of awe that I feel from time to time in many things. This book inspired tremendous hope in me.

— Pam Kent
Kent Management Inc.

***

Some focus on darkness, while some focus on light. What you chose to see will change your life. Jordan Allen chose the light long before physicians discovered the incurable brain tumor. That Choice unlocked the doors to Heaven giving him an unprecedented peek into the Kingdom. Jennifer Johnson shares the light that Jordan brought back from Heaven in her spirit-touching book, ***The Kingdom Child***. ***The Kingdom Child*** melts the coldest heart and opens the blindest of eyes. If you are looking for a book that brings a message from God, you have found it.

- R. H. Lewis, author of ***Missing Pieces, Josh, Keith,*** and ***Sarah,*** weaving Christ's life-changing Power into adventures, mysteries, and thrillers.

***

"When Jordan prayed, "God, help me be all that you need me to be," he didn't know he was asking for a brain tumor. At fourteen, it would seem he had his whole life ahead of him, and he did. Because of that prayer, God used Jordan to touch hearts and change lives through the power of His Holy Spirit. We see only a small piece of God's design. What if we could see the whole picture? Jennifer Johnson has done a beautiful job of penning Jordan's journey as a Kingdom Child and revealing such truths as "There is a life that leads to death, and a death that leads to life." A truly touching story. If it causes you to see those around you and become concerned about their fate, then God is still using Jordan."

~Diane Yates, author of *Pathways of the Heart* and *All That Matters*

***

This is a God-inspired, Spirit-led work. For the churched, convicting and challenging! The hard question is not only do you believe, but are you willing to live out your faith; really do and endure whatever it takes to become who God wants you to be? For the unchurched, it is a glimpse of who God is and what His promise of an abundant life looks like, both in the here and now, and thereafter. Here are possibilities of the spirit world, and that place where physical and spiritual overlap. This a cornucopia of imagery, teaching, and revelation that cries out to be read, savored, and discussed, all interwoven in the personal story of faith tested by terminal illness and what happened when a young teenager decided to let God's will for him also be his.

- TJ Szafar

***

I have read other accounts of visiting and returning to tell — patients on operating tables, comas, drowning victims, etc. — but this explains away all the doubt. Jordan gave credit to the One whom credit must be given.

You cannot say, "I don't know." You do because He lives in you and craves for you to acknowledge Him. You have purpose. It says in the book, "Each night, he would ask God 'to help him be all that he needed to be,' hoping his prayer would reveal God's plan." Through Jordan's suffering, he was and will continue to be what God needs him to be — a life preserver for the Lord's children... and we are all God's children.

I praise the Allen family and Jennifer Johnson for allowing us to experience through Jordan what it is like. It is *with Him* or *without Him*. I most definitely choose *with Him*. Fear death? Never. Romans 14:8 Whether we live or die, we are with Christ.

Thank you, Jordan. You will be bringing so many to Christ!

— CJ Loiacono

THE KINGDOM CHILD

A Fight for Survival Leads to the
Redemption of Lost Souls

Jennifer Johnson

W & B Publishers
USA

W & B Publishers

For information:
W & B Publishers
9001 Ridge Hill Street
Kernersville, NC 27284

www.a-argusbooks.com

ISBN: 9781635540802

The Kingdom Child is the true story of Jordan Allen and his family. Although the author has taken liberties in reconstructing the point of view of Jordan himself, it is based on Scripture and the information provided by the Allen family. Jennifer Johnson has written this book as authentically as possible for the betterment of mankind, as a 'fisher of men.'

Book Cover designed by Melissa Carrigee

Printed in the United States of America

Heavenly Father, I thank You for the Allen family, and for allowing me to be a part of their faith journey. Thank you for my husband, Steve, who has been a tremendous source of encouragement and strength. Thank You also for the people who have supported me and prayed over this book. May the fruits that come from it bring You glory and honor.

"I am convinced that nothing can ever separate us from his love. Death can't, and life can't. The angels can't and the demons can't. Our fears for today, our worries about tomorrow, and even the powers of hell can't keep God's love away. Whether we are high above the sky or in the deepest ocean, nothing in all creation will ever be able to separate us from the love of God that is revealed in Christ Jesus our Lord." (Romans 8:38–39)

T.S., you are truly a godsend. Thank you.

Introduction

This story reveals what a Kingdom Child is supposed to look like. It was inspired by a fourteen-year-old boy named Jordan Allen who discovered his divine purpose would be revealed while fighting for his life. At the age of thirteen, Jordan was diagnosed with an inoperable brain tumor. During this difficult time, Jordan was a picture of authentic faith when having to "walk through the valley of the shadow of death." (Psalm 23)

While in and out of a coma, Jordan was given the gift of seeing the physical world and the spiritual world as one. He learned it's not a physical death we should fear but a spiritual death, even among those claiming to be Christian. We may think we're on the pathway to Heaven when actually our own free will has led us astray.

My hope is this book will pierce the soul of every reader, causing them to look deeply into their own beliefs. It's easy to profess Christianity, but it's another thing to be all that God calls us to be, especially in our darkest moments.

Faith prepares us for every battle we face, including death. But only a Kingdom Child recognizes the real battle being fought is for the allegiance of our souls.

Table of Contents

Chapter One

When Life Turns on a Dime

Jordan's Story

"Be careful what you pray for because you may not be prepared for the answer God gives." That was the sermon our Pastor preached one Sunday morning. Looking back, I never would have guessed how one simple message would change my life forever. Here's what happened.

I dreamt of becoming a professional football player. What could be better than living the dream of playing sports, making a lot of money, and owning expensive cars and houses? Surely God wanted me to be happy, so why wouldn't my prayer come true? However, I soon discovered God had a much bigger plan in store for my life.

I grew up in a nice suburban neighborhood and my parents were strong Christians. In fact, I can't remember a Sunday we didn't attend church. Mom said being a Christian was a calling; something to be taken very seriously. "It's easier to talk-the-talk than walk-the-walk." She must have repeated that a million times to both me and my sister!

Everyone in my church looked "Christian," but I learned being a Christian was more than how we appeared on the outside. Sometimes I found Christianity confusing because many of my friends and relatives called themselves Christians, yet preferred watching football on Sunday more than attending a church service. Some would even sneak out early so they wouldn't miss kickoff. I wondered if any of them had ever read the Bible.

I guess I was different because I didn't mind going to church. I liked hearing the Pastor talk about people in the Bible, especially the young kid who killed a huge scary giant with a rock and a sling. I was also curious about demons and angels and whether or not they were real. Does the spiritual world really exist even though we can't see it?

My parents taught us every person was either on the pathway to Heaven or the pathway to Hell. There were only two destinations, and the choices we make determined which path we're on. If the Bible was so black and white about where we spend eternity, then how come I never heard a sermon about Hell? I heard lots of sermons about Heaven and the wonderful things God does for us. But what happens to us if we do something bad? And what about the devil? What's his story and why does he hate Christians so much? I once asked a pastor if he believed in Satan and was shocked to hear he didn't. How could he not believe in something God talked about in the Bible? I wondered how many others thought like him. Did pastors assume every person attending church was going to Heaven? What if there was someone in the congregation who thought he was going to Heaven but was actually on the pathway to Hell?

Every week our Sunday school class recited the Lord's Prayer and, truthfully, I never really understood what it meant. I just repeated the prayer along with everyone else. But one of the verses, "Thy will be done," got my attention, so I decided to ask my parents about it. They told me God's will represented His plan for my life. Apparently, God has a plan for everyone. I wondered if my plan and His plan were one in the same. Surely if I attended church each week and remained good in God's eyes, then my dream of playing football would come true, or would it?

One evening, I decided to add a new prayer to my list of requests. After thanking God for everything, I included, "God, help me be all that you need me to be."

Well, after several years of praying this night after night, my prayer was finally answered, but not in the way I expected. If there's one thing I've learned, faith isn't about getting what you want. Instead, it's more about accepting the answer you receive.

***

Rosalyn's Story

In the summer of 2010, my son started experiencing recurring headaches. Jordan was a healthy kid, so the doctor brushed it off on spending too much time in front of the TV. Little did we know that havoc was about to be unleashed upon our lives. These headaches went on for several weeks and we constantly found ourselves back in the doctor's office. Yet it never crossed anyone's mind Jordan was fighting for his life.

One morning the pain was so excruciating it caused Jordan to stagger into the kitchen. He gripped his head with both hands while screaming about a loud ringing sound inside his ears. We immediately jumped in the car and raced to the Emergency Room. His sister Paige held Jordan's hand as tears streamed down his cheeks. He tried to remain strong in front of his little sister while my husband, Sam, calmly reassured them everything was ok. Yet deep inside we feared something more serious was happening.

After parking the car, we quickly got Jordan inside the hospital. His balance had sev erely diminished as he cried out, "Everything is spinning. I'm going to fall!" Sam yelled for help as a team of nurses and doctors ran to our side. Sam caught Jordan just before he hit the floor. He was unconscious when doctors lifted him onto a stretcher. We watched in fear as our son disappeared through heavy metal doors at the end of the hospital corridor.

"Oh my God! Jordan, my baby!" I cried out, feeling utterly hopeless. Paige buried her face into my side as we stood motionless. A nurse appeared who seemed as devastated as we were and told us to go to the waiting room area until we heard from the doctors. Just then our older son Bear arrived at the hospital. I sobbed in his arms, while Sam told him what happened. Our world had suddenly fallen apart.

***

Jordan's Story

I remember waking up one morning with a shooting pain inside my head. My body felt like it was on a merry-go-round, spinning in every direction. I tried to walk but couldn't keep my balance. Something wasn't right. In fact, something was terribly wrong.

The dizziness and the ringing in my ears wouldn't stop. All I remembered was being rushed to the hospital and Paige holding my hand. I could feel her squeezing my arm as I tried not to throw up. I looked over at her and saw tears in her eyes.

"It's OK, Paige," I whispered, trying to be brave. But truthfully, I didn't know if I was OK. I closed my eyes, begging God to take the pain away.

We arrived at the hospital and luckily found a parking spot near the elevator. As I stepped out of the car, everything became foggy and Dad grabbed my arm, keeping me from falling.

"You got this, Jordan. Take your time." His voice was calm. Holding me close, we walked inside the building. I started to pass out before Dad caught me. He was yelling for help. I didn't know what was happening. I closed my eyes, thinking if I could just fall asleep, all this pain and confusion would all go away.

The hospital sounds around me faded and everything became black. I tried to hear what the doctors were saying, but their words jumbled together. I was lifted onto a stretcher before I passed out.

I felt my spirit lifted out of my body as it actually stood across the room, observing everything. I was wheeled to a room with a team of doctors at my side. My spirit watched intently while nurses frantically attached machines to my body. One doctor fiercely pounded on my chest while breathing into my mouth. "Come on Jordan! Come on!" My spirit could see the terror in his eyes as he stared at my lifeless body. Another doctor was looking at a monitor, yelling out numbers and orders to the nurses. Chaos had set in and everyone was in a state of hysteria.

"We're losing him!" a doctor yelled.

Was he talking about me? Was I dying? I watched in disbelief, feeling helpless. My body felt icy cold as my spirit shivered in the corner of the room, trying to grasp what was happening. I thought I was having a nightmare. A doctor tried to resuscitate me, while perspiring profusely.

"Come on, Jordan! Come on!"

After several moments, he stopped. Trying to catch his breath, he stood over me, shaking his head, as sweat dripped from his forehead. "He's not breathing. I don't have a heartbeat. We've lost him."

I looked at the machine monitoring my heart. A flat yellow line ran across the screen. The doctor stood motionless with his eyes closed. He told another doctor to go find my parents and tell them what happened. *No. I wasn't dead! This couldn't be happening!*

***

Rosalyn's Story

We waited restlessly, staring at a television. Sam was on the phone talking to his sister while Paige, Bear, and I tried to process what happened to Jordan. I stared blankly at the floor crying, anxiously waiting for any news on his condition. Then I heard a voice coming from across the room.

"Mr. and Mrs. Allen." A doctor appeared, soaked in perspiration, and by his expression, we feared the worse. He led us to a private room just outside the waiting area. Bear held Paige while Sam and I braced ourselves for whatever he was going to say. The doctor closed the door behind us.

"I'm Dr. Michaels. I'm so sorry to have to tell you this, but Jordan didn't make it."

"Oh my God! No!" I cried out. "Please tell me Jordan is OK!"

Paige began screaming, "No! Mama, no!"

Bear stood motionless, paralyzed by the news. Sam ran over and held me in his arms. "Oh my God! This didn't happen!" he said, sobbing.

***

Jordan's Story

"No! No!" My spirit shouted across the room. I tried to grab one of the doctors, but my hands went right through him as he walked out of the room. Another doctor motioned several nurses to assist. They raced in and stood over my body, looking for any sign of life. The doctor who tried to save me stared blankly at the flat line on the monitor. My spirit ran to the side of the bed hitting my body while screaming, "Wake up! Please wake up!" Nothing changed. I buried my face in my hands.

I felt a hand on my shoulder. Must be the doctor.

"Don't be afraid, Jordan. I'm right here."

That was not the doctor's voice.

I took my hands away from my eyes and turned around, but no one was there. Yet I felt as if someone had wrapped a warm blanket around my spirit. I noticed one of the nurses standing in the corner of the room, at a distance from all of the commotion.

She calmly approached my bedside, leaned over, and tilted my head back, opening my mouth with her other hand. She breathed in slowly as air filled my lungs. It felt like someone had poured warm water over me from the top of my head to my toes.

When the doctor noticed what she was doing, he angrily said, "It's too late. He's gone. I did everything I could."

The nurse ignored him. She continued to breathe into my lungs. Between attempts to resuscitate me, she whispered in my ear, "Come back, Jordan. It's not your time."

She pushed gently on my chest. Irritated, the doctor reached out to grab her. Just then, the monitor made a beeping sound. A tiny blip interrupted the flat yellow line.

I felt my lungs taking in air. A rhythmic pattern formed across the screen of the heart monitor. The doctor's face turned pale.

My body, soul, and spirit became one again. I slowly opened my eyes and saw the nurse standing over me. A bright light shone around her, so I could only see her face dimly, but I could tell she was smiling. Her eyes sparkled as she whispered, "Don't be afraid, Jordan. God always has the final say."

The doctor approached my bedside. "Oh my God, he's alive!" He checked the machines, each of which was recording a different vital sign. The nurse slipped out of his way and left the room.

"It's not possible! How could—" The doctor's words were cut off as the medical team filled my room with commotion.

"We have a pulse!" the doctor yelled out. "Get him to ICU! And somebody go tell his parents!"

A nurse raced out of the room in search of my family. Exhaustion overcame me, and I couldn't keep my eyes open. The sounds of the room faded to silence as I fell deep into a coma.

***

Rosalyn's Story

We sat quietly in the private room while the doctor went over in detail everything that happened. Jordan was gone and the next protocol was to perform an autopsy in hopes to find out what caused his death. He mentioned a possible brain tumor but wasn't certain. I kept shaking my head in disbelief, thinking this was all a bad dream. Jordan dead? How? Why? I couldn't begin to grasp even the thought of losing my son, and now having to face the reality it happened?

The door flew open and a nurse, trying to catch her breath, cried out, "He's alive! We got a pulse. Jordan is breathing. He's headed to ICU!" The doctor looked up in disbelief.

"Wait here, Mr. and Mrs. Allen. I'll be right back!" He ran out of the room with the nurse.

We couldn't believe it. Paige was jumping up and down as I fell to the ground, praising God. He saved our son! Bear hugged Sam as we all tried to catch our breath.

An hour later, Dr. Michaels returned and updated us on Jordan's condition. Jordan was in a coma, on a ventilator, but his vitals had returned. His condition was critical and the doctors weren't optimistic. We raced to his room. I couldn't wait to see him! Just before entering the ICU, Dr. Michaels recommended Sam and I go first and suggested Bear and Paige stay in the waiting area. As we approached the closed curtain, Dr. Michaels turned and looked at us.

"Mr. and Mrs. Allen, you must understand Jordan is not out the woods. His condition is very serious and you need to prepare yourself for whatever may happen to your son."

As he slowly pulled back the curtain, we gasped at what we saw. It was heart breaking. Jordan was alive, but we didn't recognize him. I grabbed Sam's hand as we stared in disbelief at machines and tubes attached to every part of his body. Sounds filled the room as monitors recorded his vitals.

"Oh my God!" It was all I could say.

The doctors ordered an MRI of his brain. It revealed a mass inside Jordan's head. The doctor told us it was cancer and by its location, the tumor was inoperable.

Devastation and hysteria set in as we stared in disbelief at the picture of a tumor around our son's brain, an image that has remained embedded in my memory. *How does a tumor like this appear out of nowhere?*

"No God! Please! Please don't let this happen!" No one is ever mentally prepared for a diagnosis of cancer, especially when it's your child. And when it strikes as quickly as it did Jordan, it's like a thief breaking into your home and stealing one of your most beloved possessions.

We were told this type of cancer had less than a five percent survival rate and that Jordan may never wake up from the coma. "Dear Lord, please save our son!" It was all I could pray as fear and despair overcame every other emotion inside me. I could barely breathe as I buried my face in my hands. Tears poured from my eyes. I knew this type of tragedy happened all the time to other families. I just couldn't believe it happened to mine. Sam was completely silent in the corner of the room. I watched him as he slowly approached the bed and gently placed his hand over Jordan's. "Hey, buddy. I love you. You're a fighter and we're here with you."

"Mr. and Mrs. Allen, Dr. Canon is Jordan's primary physician and he will be by later," Dr. Michaels said. "If you need anything, here is the call button. We're monitoring him very closely. Do you have any questions?"

"He could wake up, right?"

Dr. Michaels spoke softly as his eyes shifted to Jordan. "I don't know, Mrs. Allen. But there is a strong possibility he won't."

His words felt like a knife stuck in my heart. Twenty-four hours ago, my son was alive. Now he was in a coma, possibly facing death. The doctor left the room as we sat quietly in the dark, amazed by all the beeping sounds and lights coming from the machines. I listened to the ventilator as it pumped air into Jordan's lungs. I felt like we were living a nightmare. But this wasn't a dream. This was our new reality. For reasons beyond my understanding, God had allowed this tragedy to happen. The question was, 'Why?'

Our faith tells us God is the giver of all things. God is sovereign and He chooses when to take it all away, including life. Was this what we were facing? Would Jordan's life be unexpectedly taken away? I begged God to take my life instead of his. How could I live one day without my son? Prayer became our only defense in a battle that even the best medical professionals didn't know how to fight.

Perhaps, instead of asking why this was happening, I should be asking 'what' and 'how'? What can we learn about God from this, and how will we glorify Him in the midst of it? As a Christian, I knew these were the right questions, but my heart didn't feel right with this. If God chose to take our son, how would we be blessed? How does one worship a God of love who allows this tragedy to happen? I buried my face into my hands, taking in deep breaths. My stomach churned inside. I thought I was going to throw up. "Stay calm," I said to myself.

Paige and Bear came into the room, and Paige began to cry as she stared in disbelief at her brother. Sam reached over and gripped her hand. She buried her face in her daddy's chest, sobbing over Jordan.

"Why, Daddy, why!?" she cried out as Sam stared blankly at a wall, holding Paige tightly in his arms. There were no words to comfort her or each other. Bear walked over and gently touched Jordan's arm. He looked at me, hoping for some kind of explanation but I didn't have one. None of us could begin to fathom what happened. We sat for hours in silence, trying to wrap our heads around this turn of events. Just hours before, we were a family of five and now we faced the threat of becoming a family of four. I walked over to the window and looked outside. I could vaguely hear the sounds of the city below us over the sounds of the machines in our room. Staring out the window, I watched people walk down the street as cars pass by. How could a world appear so normal on the outside, while our world was falling apart?

I shook my head in disbelief. *No, No, this isn't happening!* I knew in my heart God could save Jordan. And I knew He would be with us, even if others abandoned us, including the doctors. What else could we cling to but His promises? If I remained in Him, He would remain in me. (John 15:4) God would be in the center of our pain, to carry us and sustain us when nothing else could.

That's when I heard a soft, gentle whisper in my heart. *Don't be afraid, Rosalyn. I'm right here.*

God wasn't watching this from Heaven. He was right here with us in the hospital. His presence was in the midst of our anguish. Although I was drowning in fear, His word said nothing could snatch Jordan from the palm of His hand, not even cancer. If God was willing, He could save Jordan. That tiny sliver of hope was my only source of strength.

"God, help me, please!" I leaned against the window as tears flowed uncontrollably down my cheeks. I clasped my hands together in prayer, taking in deep breaths, trying to gain composure. *Why would God allow something like this to happen to my family? Was this a testing of our faith? Were we being punished for something?* My thoughts were all over the place as I tried to rationalize what seemed so irrational.

This journey forced all of us to confront the depth of our faith. At the drop of a dime, life can change, and when faced with a catastrophic event, faith becomes transparent. Therefore, we must choose where our true allegiance lies. Do we truly trust God no matter what happens, or not? I must admit, the latter would have been easier.

I realized our family had to make a choice; one that I never anticipated we would ever have to face. We had to believe what we said we believed. How many times did I pound this truth into my kids? How many times did I remind them Christianity is more than talking-the-talk? Now it was my time for our family to walk-the-walk. I had to hear my own words as they echoed in my heart. The challenge for Christians is to live out our faith and be all that Christ calls us to be, especially in times of crisis. The Bible teaches us in (James 1:2-8) that our faith is to never waver but remain firm, no matter what trials come our way. Now it was my turn to practice what I preached.

I looked over at Paige and Sam. Both had fallen asleep, at least for the moment. Bear decided to head home. There were only three chairs in the room and it was very cramped. We hugged tightly and said our good byes. I watched him disappear down the hallway, feeling thankful for my oldest son. He was a great support, especially for Paige. I walked back into Jordan's room, reclined the chair and closed my eyes. A conversation I once had with Mom came to me.

She told me life was like a puzzle and God hands us each piece one at a time. Some pieces represent the good things while others represent the bad. Although our humanness can't fully understand why God allows both the good and bad pieces, our faith assures us when they are put together, a beautiful masterpiece of His divine plan will be revealed for all our lives.

Jordan's illness was a piece of life's puzzle handed to our family. I certainly didn't choose this piece. It just happened. And now we had to figure out how to make it all fit together.

Would our emotions cause our faith to be tossed like ocean waves, or would we remain firm by accepting the sovereignty of God and praising Him no matter what the outcome? It was our choice.

When Sam and Paige woke up, it was very late. Sam and I wanted Paige to go home and sleep, while someone would always be with Jordan. For now, that person was me. It was devastating to see so many other patients battling their suffering alone in their rooms. I promised Jordan he would never be alone. Besides, I wanted to be here in case he woke up. We hugged each other tightly and prayed over Jordan. I looked into Paige's eyes, reassuring her God could heal her brother. Hope was not lost. Paige forced a smile and left with her daddy.

As the hours passed in the hospital, I pulled up a chair next to Jordan's bedside, holding his cold hand. I placed another blanket on him as I sat quietly alone in the dark. If I had one wish, it was to have my simple life back just the way it was. I prayed for the tumor to miraculously vanish.

If Jordan died, would my life be swallowed up in anguish? God is the Giver of life, but He also decides when we take our last breath. Why now? Why Jordan?

The doctors lost hope as each day passed with no change in Jordan's condition. No one knew whether Jordan would live or die. Only God knew for certain and He would have the final say.

Night after night, we waited for God to answer our prayers. I opened a Bible I found in the room and began reading Psalm 23. My family was drowning in the valley of the shadow of death.

Chapter Two

God's Place of Rest

Rosalyn's Story

I don't recall sleeping as I sat quietly by Jordan's bedside watching the days turn into night, and the nights turn into days. It seemed like eternity since Jordan was admitted, but only five days had passed. I kept telling myself that our timing and God's timing are not always the same. Every day Jordan remained with us was a gift. Every breath he took was a sign of hope.

I was now living my days moment-by-moment with a renewed anticipation that Jordan might wake up. Word had gotten out about what had happened and Jordan's hospital room was filled with banners, pictures, and balloons as we waited patiently for our boy to open his eyes.

Sam returned each morning on his way to work and I would update him on the prior evening's events. We watched the hospital bustle with activity, while Jordan

slept peacefully in the midst of this chaos.
Nurses constantly raced from one room to the
next, up and down the hallway, while Sam
and I sat quietly in Jordan's room waiting on
a miracle. Paige had refused to sleep upstairs
by herself, so the two of them were now
sleeping downstairs in our master bedroom.
We agreed it would be best to keep Paige's
routine as normal as possible, although her
desire was to spend every waking moment
next to her brother. Bear was always available
to help with Paige's activities. We had to
come up with a schedule for her. I wondered
if she was being bombarded by friends asking
questions about Jordan. I tried to not cry in
front of her because we needed to be strong as
I constantly reminded ourselves God was able
to save Jordan.

I thought back on what my life was
like before this crisis occurred. I hadn't
appreciated a typical day filled with errands
and busyness until it was ripped from me. I
wondered if I would ever experience a normal
day again.

How would we manage our jobs?
How would we manage taking care of Paige
from a hospital room? Bear also had his job
and this would take a toll on him. Eventually
one of us would have to return full time to
work, while the other stayed with Jordan. As
his mother, I knew I could never leave him, so
it made sense for Sam to return to work while

I managed life from here. I had to trust God would pay our bills.

Each morning as I waited for Sam to stop in, I found it harder and harder to leave Jordan's bedside. I would have to force myself to leave the room, if only for a moment to get something to eat or just take a walk. One morning as I walked down the hospital corridor, I glanced inside each room. Every room in the ICU was occupied and I wondered how many of the patients had visitors or loved ones who frequently checked on them? Many seemed isolated from the world. What would it be like night after night to be alone in a hospital room, fighting for life? My heart hurt as I wondered about what brought them here in the first place. Perhaps life was ripped from them just as it had been from Jordan.

After I got my meal from the cafeteria counter, I chose a table in a far corner. As I wrapped my hands around a cup of coffee, a warm sensation came over me.

Heavenly Father, I prayed, *thank You for the simple pleasure of having a mundane life. I promise I will never see anything as mundane ever again. Thank You for all the days of good health You give us, however many they may be.*

***

Jordan's Story

"Jordan, can you hear me? Can you open your eyes?"

I slowly turned my head toward the unfamiliar voice. I had no idea how long I'd been asleep, but when I awoke, I was in a place I didn't recognize. It wasn't the hospital or my home. It was a place completely unfamiliar to me. I was in room placed in the center of a garden that only had three walls. The opening was like a picture window displaying God's creation from all over the world. It was like every beautiful thing He ever made was right in front of me. I looked around and felt an overwhelming sense of peace. There weren't any doctors or nurses and I wondered if I was dreaming. Radiant light filled the room, yet there wasn't a lamp in sight.

Sitting on a chair next to me was a very tall and exceptionally handsome man, and he was smiling at me. His hair was white as snow, pulled back into a long ponytail that draped over his shoulder. His skin was flawless and slightly bronzed. He wore blue jeans and a denim shirt that matched his crystal-blue eyes.

"I'm glad you're finally awake." He gently stroked my head with a warm hand. "Let me help you sit up."

I slowly sat up still feeling groggy from the deep sleep I'd been in.

The man took my hand and helped me to stand. I was nervous because the last time I tried to walk, I became so dizzy I lost my balance.

"It's okay, Jordan. You can do it."

I slowly got out of the bed and stood on my own two feet. The dizziness and ringing in my head were completely gone and I felt stronger than I ever had.

I looked through the huge opening where a wall appeared missing. It was like a window without any glass. The breeze coming in filled the room with a fragrance of roses as it gently touched my skin.

The man led me to the opening. As I looked closer at God's creation, I was blown away by all of its beauty. It's like I was seeing the things of this earth for the first time.

Flowers of every kind and color covered the land like a carpet. Just beyond the fields of flowers, I saw a vineyard with grapes so huge and plump, I could see their clusters from where I stood. To my right, I saw the ocean, and I heard waves crashing on the white-sand beaches. To my left, rivers and streams poured into a huge lake, where boats were docked and many people were fishing. There were snow-capped mountains in the distance. One stood so high that clouds covered its peak. It was the most magnificent mountain I'd ever seen, and a rainbow of lights formed a circle around its base.

Multiple stone pathways went off in different directions, like a maze. Just beyond the pathways, a narrow, winding road led up to a large mountain. The road looked like it was paved with sparkling diamonds that glistened when light touched its surface.

Hundreds, maybe thousands of people wandered along the pathways, but only a handful were walking on the narrow road leading up to the mountain. Fruit trees of every kind grew along the paths, and people were picking the fruit off the trees and eating as they walked.

The man with me took a long, slow breath. "Beautiful isn't it?"

It suddenly dawned on me that I may have died. "Is this Heaven?"

He smiled. "No. The Lord has brought you to His Place of Rest."

I'd never heard of God's Place of Rest. "But I thought when Christians die, we go straight to Heaven."

"You didn't die, Jordan. The Lord delivered you from death." The man sat on the windowsill so we could look at each other face-to-face.

As I looked into his eyes, there was something very familiar about him. I felt I'd known him my whole life. "Where are my parents and my sister? Where's Bear?"

"They're at the hospital. Your body is still very sick."

"So am I like … a ghost?"

His smile widened. "No. The Lord brought you here in answer to your prayer."

"What prayer?"

He looked at me intently. "Did you not pray for God to help you be all that He needed you to be?"

"Well, yeah."

"Often a person must be removed from the world in order to understand God's divine purpose for him. Although you are still in the world, you are no longer of it."

Figuring I must be dreaming, I touched my arms and legs. They felt normal. But as I looked closer, I noticed all of my scars and freckles were gone. And my skin glistened in the light. I had on the clothes that I wore to the hospital, yet even they looked brand new.

Something deep inside felt different, like I was a new person with no disease or flaws.

As I stepped over the windowsill out onto the grass, it felt like carpet on my bare feet. The man stepped out also, taking in deep breaths of the fragrant air.

This couldn't be real. I closed my eyes tightly and said, "Wake up, Jordan!" But when I opened my eyes, the man was still there, watching me.

"You're not dreaming."

I couldn't understand what was happening. How could God's divine purpose involve my being separated from my family? I was only thirteen. "Will I ever see my parents or my sister again?" I asked, trying to hold back tears.

"Oh, yes, most certainly. In God's perfect timing." The man hugged me as though we'd known each other our whole lives.

"Are you ... Jesus?"

The man laughed. "No, Jordan. I'm your guardian angel. You can call me Michael. Jesus assigned me to protect you. I've been with you ever since the day you were born."

My eyes widened and I stepped back. As I looked at Michael, I didn't know if I should be happy or afraid.

"Why do you seem so surprised? I know you've heard about angels in church."

"Well, yeah, but I never thought I would actually see one."

Michael chuckled. "Come. Let's go for a walk." He took my hand and led me down one of the pathways. The rocks glistened in the sunlight, yet when I looked into the sky, the sun was nowhere to be found. The temperature was neither hot nor cold. It was like a perfect spring day.

As he held my hand, a warm sensation came over me. It felt familiar, yet I couldn't remember when I'd experienced it before.

As we continued down the pathway, I peeked behind his back.

"What are you looking for?" Michael asked.

"Your wings," I quietly confessed, embarrassed.

Michael stopped. "Stay here. I want to show you something." He walked about ten yards ahead of me. When he turned around to face me, a brilliant light illuminated from his body. It was so bright I had to cover my eyes. As I peeked through my fingers, Michael grew to over twenty feet tall. He spread out his arms, and his wings filled the sky. His hair changed from white to golden, his eyes sparkled like emeralds, and he wore a long, white, glistening robe. He was the most beautiful being I had ever seen. His appearance was so overpowering, I fell to the ground and hid my face, trembling with fear.

"Don't be afraid, Jordan. The Lord's favor is upon you." In an instant, his image turned back to the man I'd originally met. He reached down, offering his hand to help me stand.

I was speechless and still shaken by his transformation. But when our fingers touched, my fear vanished and a sense of peace came over me.

"You never need to be afraid, Jordan. The Lord sends His angels to protect those who call on His name. I'm here to protect you because of your faithfulness and obedience to God. Now, let's go get something to eat. I know you must be hungry."

As we walked along, I saw all different kinds of fruit hanging from the tree branches. There were apples, oranges, lemons, and fruits I didn't recognize. The bluest sky I'd ever seen appeared above the trees, and rays of light poured between the branches, yet the source of the light was still a mystery. Birds sang all around me, and animals of every species grazed with one another, and not one seemed afraid of being attacked. I actually saw lambs eating with lions.

This Place of Rest reminded me of the story of Adam and Eve in the Garden of Eden. I wondered if that garden was anything like this, a place where predator and prey were united. I reached up to grab one of the apples from a tree branch, but then hesitated.

"Go ahead. They're for your enjoyment," Michael said smiling.

I may have been just a spirit, but hunger sounds grumbled inside my stomach. As I held the apple in my hands, I noticed how shiny and perfect it was. Not one bruise or discoloration anywhere on it. I finally took a bite. The most succulent flavor I had ever tasted astonished my taste buds.

As we continued our walk, I couldn't help but stare at others wandering on the pathways. "Who are all these people?"

"Many of them are children of God, like you."

"But not all of them?"

"No."

I stared at the pathways going in all different directions, some even crossing over onto other pathways. "Do all of these roads lead to the same place?"

"No." Michael pointed to the narrow road that led up the mountain. "But with your help, many might choose the path leading to that road."

"Where does it go?"

"To the Heavenly Kingdom."

I looked at all the people on the other pathways. "Are you saying that some of these people aren't going to Heaven?"

"Only the children of God go to Heaven." Michael sighed. "As you can see, the road is narrow, and only a few will find it."

"What happens to those who don't?" I knew the answer from reading the Bible, but I still needed to hear it.

"Their souls will spend eternity in Hell." Michael said it in such a matter-of-fact way it made me realize there was no in-between. Heaven and Hell were the only two destinations these pathways would lead to.

Michael looked into the light that surrounded God's Place of Rest. "For those who receive Christ and believe in His name, He gives the right to be called children of God. The others are children of the devil."

A chill ran down my spine. I wasn't sure what to ask next, and even if I could come up with something, I was scared to hear his answer. So I remained speechless as I watched so many people wander aimlessly along the pathways. Many seemed lost and confused, like mice in a maze.

The road to Heaven could be seen from every direction. Yet some people were going in the opposite direction. I pointed to the people who looked lost. "Can't they see the road that leads to Heaven?"

"No, they can't."

"But it's so obvious! How can they miss it?"

"They see only with their eyes, not with their hearts. Soon you will understand what I mean."

Several people weren't going any-where. They had come to a fork in their pathway, and then remained at a standstill. Some of them looked afraid. "Why are they just standing there?"

"They stopped seeking. Therefore, they will never find."

I shrugged. "Well, maybe they should just ask someone for help."

Michael shook his head. "That's the problem. Asking the wrong person for help is what led them down the wrong path in the first place."

"Why don't they just ask God? This is His Place of Rest, right?"

Michael nodded. "That is the logical solution. But many people seek logic from sources other than God."

"You're an angel. Can't you help them?"

"I'm afraid not. The Lord only sends His angels to those who call on His name."

I looked up at Michael, pondering what he'd just said. "So only Christians have angels?"

"Only God decides when, where, and whom His angels are to minister. My instructions come from God and no one else," Michael stated.

My spirit was disturbed as I observed the standstills.

"How long will they stand there?"

"For many, a lifetime."

I looked at Michael in disbelief. How could anyone just stand there for a lifetime? "Will any of them find their way?"

"As long as there's breath, there's hope."

"Would God help them if they asked Him?"

"Yes, of course. But many refuse to ask God for help," Michael said with a deep sigh.

Why would anyone refuse God's help? Yet as we walked along, I was amazed at the number of people who had. "Well, they're stupid," I said, frustrated.

Michael looked at me. "Jordan, do you remember when you wanted to learn how to ride a two-wheel bike? What happened when you got on the bike all by yourself?"

"I fell hard on the cement and scraped my knee and arm."

"You wouldn't allow anyone, even your parents, to help you. Your pride prevented you from seeking help. Many of these people are the same way. They insist on living their lives without anyone's help, including God's."

"Yeah, but I was only six. I didn't know better."

"Yes, you did. You knew getting on a bike all by yourself could be dangerous. Your parents had warned you it would be, but you didn't listen."

I reflected back on that moment, remembering the warnings Mom gave me. I shrugged them off because I didn't want to be treated as child. Yet, I was a child and her warning was merely words of protection. I could still see today the hurt in Mom's eyes as I screamed for help. Yet she never said, "I told you so." Instead she picked me up, cleaned my wounds and led me into the house to get something to eat. It was a humbling moment for me.

Michael looked at me as though he could read my thoughts. "God has revealed Himself through His creation. His invisible qualities can be clearly seen by people of all ages through everything He has made. Yet still, many refuse to seek Him or even acknowledge His existence. Often humans think they can find their own way through life. But eventually they need to decide whether to seek God's help or not."

My heart ached for these people. Some were on their knees, crying, yet refusing to ask God for help. I held Michael's hand and gripped it tight.

"What's wrong?"

"I don't want to become that. Not ever. Will you always be with me?"

"The Lord will always be with you. He never abandons His children."

We stood there a long time, staring at the standstills. The answer to their problems was right in front of them, but they couldn't see it. Even worse, they didn't seek it.

"Maybe I could help them. I could show them which way to go."

Michael smiled. "Yes, Jordan, maybe you could."

"Do these people believe in God?"

"Some claim to believe, yet only know Him by name."

"What do you mean?"

"They never read the Bible. They don't take worship seriously. There are even some who deny God's existence altogether."

I knew people like that. I had friends who said they believed in Christ, yet never went to church. And some of my friends didn't believe at all. I'd never thought much about it until now.

"Which ones are the nonbelievers?"

Michael pointed to the people walking on pathways that led toward what appeared to be a mass of black clouds. "Is that Hell?"

"No. But that pathway leads to it. Their hearts have become hardened as they wandered through the darkness of life, blinded by their own ignorance."

A ray of light broke through the dark mass, casting shadows all around the people. "What is that?" I asked, pointing.

"The light is a reflection of God's love. He never abandons His children, even if they abandon Him. He is constantly trying to lead them down the right path, and He will continue to do so until they take their last breath on earth."

"Unbelievable!" I shook my head. "I would have given up on them a long time ago."

Michael raised an eyebrow. "Then we should all be thankful that you are not God."

I looked again at the standstills. "You said they believe in God. Even though they don't take worship seriously, isn't that enough?"

"They've placed their personal desires above what God wants for them. Their faith wavers in times of crisis, and when things are going well, they tend to forget about God. The kind of faith that God seeks is only found in a repentant heart."

I'd heard about repentance in church, but didn't really understand how it worked. "What is a repentant heart?"

"A repentant heart is one that turns away from sin and turns towards God, seeking Him in everything."

"What happens to those who don't repent?"

"They perish." Michael looked down, as though the words weighed heavily on his heart.

As we continued our walk, I noticed a man who looked to be in his sixties, sitting on his pathway at a fork in the road. His eyes were red and his cheeks wet. I figured he must have been crying for quite some time.

A young girl about my age crossed over to his path. She sat next to him and placed her arm around him. She spoke to him, pointing to the pathway that led to Heaven. But he looked away.

"Why won't that man listen to her?"

"The Lord often uses children to show others the way. But most adults don't listen simply because they're children."

"So what should she do?"

Michael looked at me. "What would you do?"

"I don't think I'd waste any more of my time on someone like him."

"What if the decision was life or death?"

"Well, that's different."

"Deciding which path to take is a life-or-death decision."

"But he clearly isn't listening to her."

"That's only his response today. Whether the seed of faith takes root or not is between that man and God. All He asks people to do is plant the seed."

"What do you mean?"

Michael reached into his pocket and pulled out a small cloth bag. "Here, keep these with you." He handed the bag to me.

"What's inside?"

"Open it."

I loosened the drawstring and saw that the bag contained a handful of tiny brown seeds, not much bigger than a pinhead. "What are these?"

"Mustard seeds. They represent the size of a person's faith before he enters the Kingdom of Heaven."

"But they're so small."

Michael nodded. "Many claim to be Christians, but the depth of their faith is smaller than one of those seeds."

I observed the people who wandered about in a futile state. "I guess I've never seen a person's faith the way God does."

Michael touched my arm. "This is the beginning of God's purpose for your illness. He is giving you a gift to be able to see inside the souls of His children. You will be able to see people's faith from a spiritual perspective. You will also see evil as it truly exists. Everything in the world will look different because you will see things through the eyes of a Kingdom Child."

I looked up at Michael trying to take in what he just said. I'd never been called a Kingdom Child. *What did this mean? Is this the answer to my prayer? Was I even capable of being a Kingdom Child?* I had so many questions, but for now I kept them inside.

I poured a few of the seeds into the palm of my hand. "What am I supposed to do with these?"

Michael gazed at the seeds as if they were priceless jewels. "Plant each one into the heart of someone God brings across your path."

"How do I do that?"

"The Lord will lead you. Trust Him fully and He will guide your steps." Michael pointed to the girl who was speaking to the elderly man. "Just like her."

"But how can I plant the seed of faith in others if I'm stuck in a hospital bed?"

Michael crouched down so he could look directly into my eyes. "Jordan, do you trust God completely?"

"Well, yeah, I think I do." But truthfully, I wasn't sure if I did.

"Then perhaps it's time to see for yourself how God is going to use you." Michael took my hands in his. "Are you ready?"

"Where are we going?"

In that moment, I felt like I was floating. I couldn't open my eyes. But something deep inside told me I was leaving God's Place of Rest.

***

Rosalyn's Story

Despite witnessing the miracle of Jordan's life being restored, the doctors held no hope that Jordan would ever wake up from his coma. Although God had brought Jordan back to life, the medical team constantly reminded us there was no cure for this type of cancer, and most likely Jordan would remain in a vegetative state. In fact, the doctors were so certain Jordan was going to die, they wouldn't even consider any treatment options.

We begged the doctors not to give up, to give God a chance, but they couldn't grasp the idea of a divine cure.

How could such brilliant minds abandon so quickly the notion of a Creator, a higher level of intellect, who had already delivered our son from death once? Why couldn't they believe God could save Jordan again? Perhaps, after witnessing so many patients die, their hearts had become hardened against the notion of a miracle.

However, I reminded myself, it's not miracles that produce faith, but rather faith that produces miracles. Sam and I believed in God's sovereignty, and we continued to pray fervently for Him to save our son. Man isn't the expert at saving lives. So our hearts remained with the Great Physician, who had the power to bring life back to the dead. He'd done it once. He could do it again. Although it appeared Jordan's body was perishing, no CAT scan could show a picture of his soul receiving new life.

Chapter Three

The Mustard Seed

Rosalyn's Story

Nurses constantly entered our room around the clock, while my husband Sam and I sat quietly and waited for Jordan to wake up from his coma. The doctors remained pessimistic about Jordan's future. Nonetheless, we refused to give up hope so quickly. They didn't know God. To them, Jordan was just another statistic whose prognosis was based on past outcomes of other patients with this type of brain tumor.

So as days passed, we sat quietly in a cold, dark hospital room waiting to see what God was going to do. It seemed like eternity since Jordan was admitted, but I kept reminding myself that our timing and God's timing were not always the same. This event drastically changed our perspective on life. Every day Jordan remained with us was a gift. Every breath he took was a sign of hope. Life became more precious as my faith became more priceless. I thought back on what my life was like just days before this crisis occurred. The simple tasks of grocery shopping, cleaning the house, or cooking dinner were things I used to gripe about. In fact, a typical day filled with errands was something I had never fully appreciated until it was ripped from me. Sam and I faced a new life filled with sleepless nights in a hospital chair, waiting for our son to wake up. We never wanted Jordan to be alone so we created shifts throughout the day and night so that either Sam or I would always be by Jordan's bedside.

As I stared quietly at the monitors displaying all of Jordan's vital signs, I began thinking about our daughter Paige and how this must be affecting her. We had to remain strong for her sake and Jordan's, but this wasn't going to be an easy task.

Heavenly Father, I'm so afraid to lose Jordan. Please help us. I need to hear Your voice.

***

Jordan's Story

When I opened my eyes, my spirit was standing in the middle of a hospital corridor with Michael right beside me. As I watched the nurses and doctors walk in and out of each room, a feeling of uneasiness came over me. Yet my guardian angel took my hand and I felt relieved.

"Come, Jordan." We strolled slowly to the end of the hallway. Above a set of huge metal doors was a sign that said Intensive Care Unit. Michael squeezed my hand as we passed through the huge metal doors without even opening them. I stood there for a moment staring at the doors, amazed by what just happened.

"I can walk through doors without opening them?"

"Remember, Jordan, you're not the same person you once were, both physically and spiritually."

The rooms were all filled with patients. A door at the end of the hallway had my name written on it. It was closed, so I couldn't see what was inside. My stomach felt queasy. A part of me wanted to return to God's Place of Rest, but I was also curious to know what was on the other side of that door. As I reached for the metal handle, Michael grabbed my hand.

"Jordan, what you're about to see will be hard to understand. But in times like these, you must trust God. This is all part of His divine plan for you."

Fearful over what I was about to discover, I looked into Michael's eyes. The confidence I saw in him gave me strength. Michael took my hand as we passed through the door. Sitting in the corner of the room was my dad. I ran over to hug him but stopped, remembering what Michael said. He looked at me with such deep compassion.

"He really can't see or hear me?"

Michael nodded. I turned back to look at Dad and noticed his eyes were staring blankly at the bed.

As I turned to look, I felt like the wind had been knocked out of me, overwhelmed by what I saw. I was lying in a hospital bed. Machines were attached to every part of my body, monitoring any vital sign still left in me. I didn't even look like myself. My face was swollen and my body seemed thin. I began to cry over the reality of what had happened to me and my family. Michael walked over and placed his arms around me. I buried my face into his chest.

"Am I dead?" I whispered.

"No, you are very much alive." Michael wiped the tears from my cheeks. "Your faith has delivered you from death."

Mom entered the room and joined Dad, who reached out and placed his arm around her as they stared at my body. It was all too surreal to believe. After a knock at the door, a doctor entered the room. My parents looked up, but remained by my bedside.

"Mr. and Mrs. Allen, my name is Dr. Canon. I'm overseeing the care for your son Jordan. I wanted to come by and introduce myself and see if you had any questions for me?"

Dad was irritated by the doctor's question. Dr. Canon's tone seemed so matter-of-fact, as though he was discussing the weather. After a long moment of silence, Dad finally spoke. "Why aren't you allowing anyone to treat Jordan?"

The doctor hesitated. "In all due respect, Mr. Allen, I have seen this type of cancer multiple times and the survival rate is less than five percent. I'm so sorry, but I don't see how Jordan could possibly survive this."

Mom looked up, trying to maintain her composure. Her hands were trembling as she choked back her tears. "Dr. Canon, this is our son! God will have the final say, not you!"

Dad took her hand. I had never seen either of my parents so upset before now. My spirit hurt so badly I thought I was going to become ill.

"Mrs. Allen, I know how difficult this must be for you, but—

"Dr. Canon, have you ever been in our shoes?" Mom asked. "If this was your child, would treatment be delayed?"

The doctor stood there, speechless.

"You have no idea what we're going through!" Mom glared into his eyes; her expression filled with anger and despair.

I so badly wanted to run into her arms and tell her everything would be okay; that I have a guardian angel right here with me; that I've seen a place called God's Place of Rest; that my body may be dead, but my spirit is alive! I wanted to scream out, "Here I am!" But I couldn't. I looked up into Michael's eyes, and by his expression, only he could hear all my cries pouring out from my heart. I'd never felt more helpless than I did at that moment. I stood there frozen, watching and feeling like my world was falling apart.

Dr. Canon stood there silent, staring at my parents.

"I don't think we have any more questions for you," my father said, shaking his head in disbelief.

Dr. Canon typed in some notes on the computer next to my bed then walked out the door. Michael walked over to my bedside and sat down. He lifted my spirit and placed me in his lap. My parents remained in the corner of the room, holding each other.

"So, dying here in the hospital is God's plan?" I asked, trying to hold back my tears.

"Who said you're going to die?"

I turned to look at Michael. "Didn't you hear what the doctor said? This type of cancer had less than a five percent survival rate. Look at me! Of course I'm dying!"

"Jordan, who do you trust more, man or God?"

I thought I trusted God more, but the doctor seemed so certain.

"But the doctor said…"

Michael reached inside my shirt pocket and took out the pouch of seeds he had given me earlier.

"Hold out your hand," Michael said as he gently placed one tiny seed into my palm. "Is your faith the size of this mustard seed?"

For a moment, I was silent. I guess I really didn't know. I didn't want to believe my faith was smaller than that tiny little seed but now it actually appeared much smaller. The doctor's diagnosis seemed so certain.

"The Lord delivered you once from death, Jordan. Do you believe He can deliver you again?"

Just then, I remembered the moment in the hospital when a nurse resuscitated me. Something about her seemed so familiar. Her eyes had sparkled just like Michael's.

"Michael, did an angel save me that day?"

"*The Lord* saved you that day. Angels are only divine instruments God uses. But you didn't answer my question, Jordan. Do you believe God can deliver you again from death?"

"But it's *cancer*. I have a *brain tumor*, and in most cases others have died," I stated.

Michael gazed at me as though he was looking into my heart. "Just answer the question, Jordan."

I started to cry because I truly didn't believe in God as much as I believed in what the doctor said.

"Faith is trusting in what we cannot see, not what we can see." He then held me close as I buried my face into his shirt. "You see that tiny little seed?" Michael gently opened up my fingers that had formed a tight fist, clutching to the seed inside.

"Under the right conditions, this little mustard seed can produce a plant nearly ten feet tall," Michael said. "Would you like your faith to be the size of a ten foot tall plant?"

I stared at that seed for a moment trying to picture in my mind a plant taller than me growing from something so small. I turned around and looked at my parents, amazed by their faith as I watched them praying over me.

"Will you help me, Michael? Will you help me to have more faith?" I pleaded.

"God will help you. He will give you *all* that you need. But the plant can only grow under certain conditions; the same is true of your faith."

"What are those conditions?"

"To love God more than anything else and to fully trust and obey Him."

"But I'm scared, Michael."

"Cancer has no claim on your life. Therefore, you don't have to fear it because cancer doesn't determine the number of days you have on this earth. Only God determines that. Only Christ has a claim on your life. Do you trust God fully with your life, no matter what happens?"

I sat quietly listening to everything Michael was saying. I looked over at my parents who were still praying over me. Tears were streaming from Mom's eyes as she begged God to save me.

"I want to, Michael," I whispered with tears in my eyes. "I want to trust Him completely."

As Michael's arms embraced me, I felt my spirit being renewed with a sense of strength and comfort I hadn't felt before; it became clear, my lifeless earthly body was only a shell over the true source of my life. Although my earthly body was sick, my spirit was alive and well.

"Will my family be OK?"

Michael smiled. "Oh yes, Jordan, they most certainly will."

I climbed off his lap and walked over to my bedside. Through a tiny opening in the hospital robe, a cord from a machine monitored my heart rate. I set the mustard seed over my heart.

"It starts with me, Michael," I said tears welling in my eyes. "I have to have faith the size of a mustard seed before I can help others. I see that now."

Michael stood behind me and placed his hands on my shoulders. He quietly said, "Praise God, Jordan. Today your mustard seed of faith has taken root."

At that moment, I felt my spirit departing from the hospital. I closed my eyes, trying to understand all that was happening to me. But something deep inside reminded me of Michael's words; to love the Lord with all my heart. I needed to trust God completely and I needed to obey Him. No matter what happened, that's what I was going to hold on to.

Chapter Four

The Devil is Real

Rosalyn's Story

The days and nights became one as we waited for any sign of life from Jordan. Sleep was a luxury, something that I longed for but could not do while in the hospital. Doctors and nurses entered our room every hour to take vital signs and I was grateful that Jordan slept through all of this. Perhaps, in his state of unconsciousness, God was protecting him from the havoc surrounding us. I hoped Jordan was dreaming happy things, completely unaware of the darkness that had submerged into our lives.

"Jordan, can you hear me, baby?" I whispered. "Mommy and Daddy love you so much. Keep on fighting, baby. God can save you, Jordan. Just believe in Him with all your heart."

I squeezed his hand, hoping for some kind of response. There was nothing. His hand was so cold, but something about his expression seemed warm and peaceful. I pulled my chair up next to his bed and rested my head against his arm. I closed my eyes for a minute trying to make sense of everything that was happening.

"God, please help me survive this. I'm so scared of losing my son. Please, God, please don't take him."

At that moment, three angels appeared, praying over Jordan and Rosalyn.

***

Jordan's Story

When I returned to God's Place of Rest, I found myself sitting alone under a tree alongside a riverbed. Some ducks rested in the tall grass on the opposite side.

I sat quietly trying to understand everything that happened. It began with a simple prayer asking God to help me be all that He needed me to be. Now, I had a brain tumor and was in coma. Yet despite my condition, God was going to use me to further His kingdom on earth.

I touched my arms and legs; they felt real. Spiritually, I was healthy and strong, sitting by a river bank in a Heavenly realm called God's Place of Rest. Strangely, I felt safe here. I didn't think about dying or having cancer. This place was comforting and quite peaceful. Fruits and vegetables grew everywhere and the people lived off the land. There were vineyards in the distance and I could see people picking the fruits and working in the fields. While sitting here, my physical condition seemed like a bad dream from a long time ago. But this wasn't a dream. Michael said this was all part of God's plan for my life. I took in a deep breath, filling my nostrils with the aroma of roses, but when I looked around, there weren't any near me.

I watched the river as it flowed gently towards a big lake where many people were fishing. I stared at my reflection in the water and began to feel thirsty. While splashing water on my face, I heard a sound behind me. I sensed someone was there, but when I turned around, I saw nothing but leaves and grass blowing in the breeze.

"Michael, is that you?" I called out, but got no answer. I passed it off as the wind rustling through the trees. As I edged closer to the water, I heard the rustling sound again. This time, I felt uneasy. "Who's there?" I called out. Again, no one answered me.

I tried not to think about it.

I felt a tingling up my spine as I looked up and saw a tall dark, faceless black shadow standing over me. "Hello, Jordan," it said in a low muffled voice.

"Who are you?" I asked, startled by its appearance. Somehow I knew I was speaking to the Devil himself. "What do you want? Where's Michael?" I felt more frightened by the minute.

"Yes, that's a good question. Where's Michael, your guardian angel?" He scoffed. "Surely you don't believe Michael can save you, do you Jordan?"

"Get away from me!"

"Don't be deceived, Jordan," Satan replied. "You're going to die."

I tried to get up and run, but the devil grabbed my ankle and I fell to the ground. I felt paralyzed with fear unable to escape its grasp. "Get away from me!" I screamed.

"Jordan, do you want to see what cancer looks like? Do you want to see the tumor that's going to kill you?"

I tried to kick him, but couldn't get away.

"Don't try to fight me, Jordan. You won't win. Look at me, Jordan. See the cancer living in you."

I was kicking as hard as I could, unable to escape from his grip. Just then, the Devil lifted the black hood off its head, revealing the most grotesque image I'd ever seen. His face oozed with worms and his eyes were filled with blood. When he laughed, blood and mucus poured from his mouth.

I began crying hysterically.

Out of nowhere came a soft, still voice. *Grab the rock, Jordan.*

I turned onto my side and saw a boulder.

Grab the rock and hold onto it.

I rolled over onto my stomach and grabbed the rock, clenching it with both hands. The Devil continued to pull on my ankles, still laughing at me.

"Oh, God, please make it go away! Save me, Jesus!" I screamed with all my might.

As if shocked by an electric current, the devil released me from his grip.

Sweating profusely, I was too terrified to look up. After lying there with my eyes closed for what seemed like a long time, I heard Michael's voice behind me.

"Jordan, it's OK. I'm here."

I opened my eyes, relieved to see my guardian angel kneeling next to me. I got up and we hugged for quite some time.

"Was that…?" Trembling with fear, I buried my face into Michael's chest. I was terrified the devil might still be around.

"That was the Enemy, Jordan."

"But aren't we in God's Place of Rest? Why was he here?"

"Darkness can exist in all holy places, except Heaven."

"But why would God allow that?"

"God allows the Devil to rule over mankind. But his power is limited and he must ask God for permission before laying a hand on one of God's children."

"I've never seen anything more frightening in my life, Michael. It was awful."

"You've been given a gift. You can see a sliver of both the physical world and the spiritual world."

I sat for a moment, taking in what he'd said. "But what if I don't want to see it? What if I don't want this gift!?" I cried out, tears flowing down my cheeks.

"Even if it meant helping you to be all that God calls you to be? Isn't that what you've been praying for?"

"I don't understand. Why does God want to scare me?" I asked, still trembling from the experience.

"God doesn't want to scare you. He wants to teach you how to rely on His strength and His courage when you face the enemy or any trial in your life. Fear is often a weapon the Devil uses to cause one's faith to waver. The only thing you ever need to fear is the Lord."

"Yeah, but I'm a Christian!"

"And being a Christian makes you more of a threat to the devil. The Enemy's mission is to destroy lives of both believers and nonbelievers. No one on earth is exempt from evil. In fact, Christians are the ones

Satan is most concerned about. Nonbelievers don't pose as much of a threat to him. Satan will work desperately to try to destroy your faith and the faith of others. However, the power in you through faith can destroy his mission."

"So he's real," I said, the thought boggling my mind. "He's a real live created being."

"He was once God's most beautiful and majestic angel in Heaven, but his pride overtook him. He wanted to be God. And because of his disobedience, Satan was cast down to earth and is allowed to rule until Christ returns."

"Why don't pastors talk about this? Shouldn't they warn us about him?"

"Yes, they should. But not all pastors, preachers, or even priests are equipped in overcoming evil."

"What do you mean?"

"Sadly, many leaders in the church don't even believe in the existence of the devil or in spiritual warfare. And the one's that do believe are often more concerned about offending their congregation than they are about teaching how to defend oneself against the devil. Sadly, so many sermons only cover part of the Bible, leaving people ill equipped to face the battles in this world."

Just then, I thought back to a conversation with my pastor. He, too, didn't believe in the Devil. I shook my head in disbelief. "How can anyone not believe? I've never been so afraid of anything in my life. Not even cancer!"

"Choosing what to believe and what not to believe in the Bible is a very dangerous thing to do," Michael stated shaking his head. "All the schooling in the world doesn't make one a Christian. That's where many pastors and priests fall short. They think once they achieve a certain level of Biblical intellect, they become converted. But conversion doesn't happen like that. In fact, our own human intellect can result in leading one astray. Remember, Jordan, everything written in the Bible is true. God cannot lie."

"I will, Michael. I promise. But where in the Bible does it teach me how to be braver?"

Michael smiled as he placed his arm around me. "The Enemy has been given a vast amount of power. But it's restricted. He wants you to be afraid and ignorant of the armor God gives you to stand up against him. Satan is a liar and a deceiver. Never doubt the power that lives in you. The Holy Spirit is far greater than any of the powers of the world."

I looked around, wanting to make sure the devil really was gone. "He told me I would die. He said the cancer would kill me."

"Jordan, your life belongs to Christ, and God has ordained the number of days you have on earth. Do not fear the one who can take the body. Fear instead the one who can take your body, soul, and spirit. Only Christ can do that."

"But I was so afraid! It was the most terrifying thing I've ever seen."

"When we fear what we see, we begin to question what we don't see," Michael explained.

"I wish I could be brave like you."

"But you are! My strength is not my own," Michael replied. "My strength comes from the Holy Spirit, the same Spirit that lives in you."

"But I could never be as courageous as a guardian angel."

"Humanly speaking, that's true. But with God, nothing is impossible. It's your faith that saved you. When you called out to Jesus, it was the demon who ran away in fear. The Holy Spirit is your strength and protection from the darkness. Do you believe me, Jordan? Do you believe the power of the Holy Spirit is greater than the power of the devil?"

I thought about everything he was saying. It was hard to believe that faith alone could save me from something so terrifying. "Will he come back?"

"*Oh yes*, he *will* come back. Satan doesn't want God's Kingdom to advance and will do everything in his power to stop you from fulfilling God's purpose. You see, the enemy is threatened by your faith. He knows the power in you is greater than the power in him. Never doubt, Jordan. Your faith must *never* waver. Do you believe in what I'm saying?"

"Yes, Michael, I do. But it's hard."

"What's hard?"

"To be strong in my faith when I feel so powerless and afraid."

Michael sat down on the ground as we watched several animals gather across the river. There was a baby lamb resting with its mother and just a few yards away, a female lion licked her paws and rolled in the grass.

"Why is the mother lamb not afraid of the lion eating her or her baby?" Michael asked.

"I don't know. On earth, that baby would have been toast a long time ago."

"The lamb's fear rests with God and not with the lion," Michael responded. "It fears nothing except God and believes in the sovereignty of God. And the lion trusts in God to fulfill all his needs, even hunger. The lamb can rest in God's peace, knowing she and her child are always under His protection."

"So if the lion ate the baby lamb, the mother lamb would be okay with it?"

"Her love for God and her trust in His sovereignty is far greater than her love for her child."

I thought about what Michael said and wondered if my parents loved God more than me and Paige. "The animals are more faithful than we are," I said laughing under my breath.

"Humans have a difficult time accepting things they cannot understand. But God's wisdom and His ways are beyond our reach. Therefore, we must trust and obey in Him. When you choose to place God over everything else in your life including your fears, you receive His peace that surpasses all understanding. You fear nothing, not even death."

"So did God allow the enemy to come to me?"

"Yes," Michael said matter-of-factly.

"I wish He wouldn't do that anymore."

"Jordan, trials can build strength and perseverance. Suffering can make us more dependent upon God than on ourselves. When we fully accept that God allows trials, then we should pray for God to use afflictions to strengthen our faith. It's one thing to call yourself a Christian. It's another thing to actually believe in what you're professing."

I paused for a moment, trying to hold back my tears. I didn't know if I really believed. My fear was so paralyzing in the moment I was face to face with the Devil, it was hard to imagine something inside of me bigger than my fear of the evil one. And deep down inside I had another fear; a fear far greater than my fear of evil.

"I'm scared about dying, Michael. Is that horrible?"

"No, it's perfectly natural. But have faith in God. He can fill you with the strength and courage to overcome any obstacle, including your fear of death. There's a life that leads to death and a death that leads to life. Soon you will understand the significance of that."

"So was God disappointed in me for being afraid?"

Michael laughed and placed his arm around me. "No, you didn't disappoint God at all. In fact, it pleases the Lord when His children cry out to Him. The Holy Spirit instructed you to call out Jesus' name, and you did."

"So Jesus' name alone causes the Enemy to go away?"

"It's not His name alone, but your faith in the power behind it."

Just then, I remembered hearing that voice in my head, telling me to grab hold of the rock. I looked over at the rock and noticed water was now pouring out from it.

"Michael, something inside told me to grab that rock, and now water is coming out from it," I said curiously. I'd never seen water flow from a rock before.

Michael turned to look at the rock and smiled.

"What does it mean, Michael?"

"Jesus is the rock of your salvation. He is your protector. Just as the water pours out from the rock, Jesus' love pours out upon His children. Soon this will all make sense to you."

"So if I see the enemy again, Jesus will make him run away?"

"Yes, Jordan. As a believer, you have the same power in you as the disciples you read about in the Bible," Michael responded.

"Am I more powerful than the Devil?"

"No, but God is, and His power lives in you. However, don't rejoice about scaring demons away. Rejoice that your name is written in the Book of Life. You're a Kingdom Child."

"Michael, can I ask one more question?"

"Of course."

"Can I drink the water from the river?" I asked, feeling very thirsty.

Michael laughed. "Most certainly. Drink as much as you need."

I reached down and cupped my hands, enjoying every moment of the cool water against my skin. It almost tasted sweet. I had never had water so refreshing.

***

Rosalyn's Story

Late one night after the new shift had just taken over, I called in one of the nurses and asked if she would stay with Jordan so I could get something to drink. While I was gone, the nurse proceeded to check all of Jordan's vital signs and fluids.

"Jordan, don't hang on. It's better if you died," the nurse whispered in his ear.

"Is everything ok?" I asked.

At the sound of my voice, she quickly turned around and looked nervously at me. "Jordan is doing fine." She typed some notes into the computer and quickly left our room.

I hovered near the doorway and watched her walk down the hallway. She stopped at the nurse's station. "I think it's horrible to let that young boy suffer," she told another nurse. "It's inhumane for his parents to keep him alive!"

Jesus and Michael stood at the nurse's station listening to the conversation taking place. "Unbelievable," Michael said, shaking his head.

"Come, let's go. The harvest is plenty and the workers are few," Jesus responded. They both disappeared down the hospital corridor.

Shivering, I returned to the chair beside Jordan's bed and stared at the flickering lights on the machines. I wondered if I'd heard the nurse correctly, telling Jordan to go ahead and die. My first impulse was anger. She, too, had given up on my son. Sitting there quietly, I shook my head in disbelief, feeling alone and scared. Something startled me and I jerked up. A tall dark shadow stood in the corner of the room. Was I delirious from lack of sleep? I pulled my blanket up close to my face. When I looked again, the shadow was gone. Dismissing it as my imagination, I placed my head on Jordan's arm, hoping sleep would come, praying Jordan would wake up.

Chapter Five

The Messenger

Rosalyn's Story

I stopped wearing a watch; the time of day
was irrelevant to me. Hours were measured
by lightness and darkness that entered our
hospital room through a small window. Days
went by fast, but the nights never seemed to
end. Sleep only occurred when I was alone in
the room with Jordan, although that didn't
happen often; nurses were in every hour
checking his vitals.

"Good morning Mrs. Allen." It was
Dr. Canon coming by to see if there had been
any change in Jordan's condition. He
normally stopped by in the morning and
before leaving for home at the end of the day.

"Good morning." I watched him
record all the vital signs and read the updates
on Jordan's condition from his nursing staff.

"Mrs. Allen, will your husband be by
this morning?"

"Yes, but why are you asking?" I wondered if the doctor had some kind of personal agenda.

"I think it would be best if we all met privately to discuss the future protocol in the care of your son," Dr. Canon responded.

"I don't know what you mean by that, Dr. Canon. As far as I can tell, no attempts are being made to try to save Jordan's life."

"Mrs. Allen, I'm so sorry to tell you, Jordan isn't making any progress. At some point, we need to discuss our next steps."

I stood there motionless. *What does he mean by 'next steps'? Was he thinking about ending Jordan's life!* His words hit me like the wind being knocked out of my lungs. Then there was another knock outside our door.

"Hey, Ros. Hey, Jordan." It was my sister Marcie who came by with breakfast.

Dr. Canon introduced himself.

"Marcie," I said, trying desperately to hold back my tears, "Dr. Canon wants to know how much longer we plan to keep Jordan alive!"

Marcie's mouth dropped at my words.

"Dr. Canon, we are on God's timetable, not yours! Perhaps that's a question you should ask God and not me!" I said, my body shaking as every emotion poured out from anger to fear to desperation.

"Mrs. Allen, every day that goes by, Jordan's body gets weaker and weaker. Never in my experience has anyone survived this kind of tumor. Even if he did survive, it may have created permanent brain damage."

"What does that mean?"

"By looking at its location, Jordan could be paralyzed. He may never be able to chew food again or breathe on his own. Nothing is certain except the severity of this tumor," Dr. Canon said. "I'm only suggesting that we consider all of our options for Jordan's sake."

"You're fired," I stated firmly, trying to hold it together.

"Excuse me?" Dr. Canon said.

"You're fired. I want a new doctor to oversee Jordan's care. You're no longer welcome in this room!"

Marcie gasped.

"I will leave now, Mrs. Allen. But when your husband comes, we should at least talk." Dr. Canon quickly left the room.

"Rosalyn," Marcie said, "maybe the doctor wants you to hear all of Jordan's options."

I glared at her. "Ending Jordan's life before God's ordained time will *never* be an option! You don't know what you're talking about! And if you don't support me and Sam, you shouldn't be here either!" With that, I felt nauseated. I sat down holding my head in my hands as tears poured from my eyes. "God, why is this happening to me?"

Marcie stood there in silence before walking over to Jordan's bedside and kissed Jordan's forehead.

"Of course I support you and Sam, but at some point, you have to look at the whole picture," Marcie responded.

"Oh, so you know Jordan's future?" I asked sarcastically.

"You know that's not what I mean. Look, I know you're tired. You haven't slept in days. Just think about it. What if God doesn't save Jordan? Or even if He does, what kind of life will Jordan have?"

"It's not a question of whether Jordan lives or dies. What's upsetting me is this hospital has already decided Jordan is going to die. They won't give him radiation or chemo. As his mother, I need to know we did everything possible to try to save him, and this medical team refuses to even try. What if Jordan was an exception? What if he fell into the five percent who survive this type of tumor?"

There was nothing left to say. The silence between us seemed like it lasted a lifetime.

Finally Marcie spoke. "Is Sam on his way?"

"Yes."

"OK, I'll be back in a little while. Try to eat something, OK?" Marcie left our room.

For the first time, I'd never felt more alone. My own family was turning against me. Was I crazy to keep Jordan alive? Were we doing the right thing?

Oh God, I need to hear Your voice. Please, tell me what to do.

I silently prayed to myself. Feeling a chill in the room, I wrapped my blanket around me and curled up in a chair. I was thankful Jordan couldn't hear any of this. I thanked God for protecting Jordan from everything happening around him.

When Sam showed up, he looked absolutely joyful. "Baby, you'll never believe what just happened!" He sat next to me and told me something astonishing.

Sam always came by just before work so he could spend some time with Jordan. That morning, after grabbing a muffin from the hospital cafeteria, he walked to the elevator. The lobby was filled with people. He watched patients walking alongside medicine stands as tubes continuously pumped fluids in their bodies. Sam noticed family members on their cell phones giving updates to loved ones. Other people paced, perhaps waiting on someone in surgery. All of these people had one thing in common: life had unexpectedly changed for both patients and loved ones without any explanation.

Sam shook his head in disbelief as he walked towards the elevators. While he waited, a tall, thin black man approached him. He wore a colorful cap on his head. The two men looked at each other and smiled politely. When the elevator doors opened, both men got in. They were the only ones in the elevator, and they were both going to the same floor.

"Are you visiting someone?" Sam asked.

"Yes, I am," the man replied in a strong British accent and gave Sam a soft smile.

"Where are you from?"

"Nigeria."

"You've come a long way." No longer interested in idle chat, Sam stared at the numbers as the elevator climbed up to the fourteenth floor.

The man looked right at Sam and said softly, "Your son will live."

"What did you say?"

"Your son will live," he repeated.

How could this man know about Jordan?

The elevator doors opened to the ICU floor. The Nigerian man stepped out, then turned around and smiled at Sam. "I believe this is your floor." He held the door open.

Sam got off the elevator, tears welling in his eyes. He hugged the Nigerian man. "Thank you," he whispered.

"No, thank God for everlasting life." The man disappeared down the hallway.

Questions raced through Sam's mind. Had God sent him an angel? Were his words true? Would Jordan live?

"I know it sounds crazy," Sam told me. "But I think this man from Nigeria was a messenger from God."

I broke into tears and hugged my husband. Just moments before, I was praying for an answer and God gave it to me. He heard my cries. For the first time in days, my tears were tears of joy.

Chapter Six:

A Call To Be Different

Jordan's Story

While Michael and I walked along the river bank, I noticed many people fishing near the shore while fishermen prepared their boats for sail. In the distance was a young girl sitting alone on one of the docks. Looking closer, I realized I recognized her. She was the same girl I saw earlier who tried to comfort the man crying on the pathway. Her feet dangled in the water, splashing the dragonflies who were flying over the surface looking for food.

"Her name is Sarah," Michael said as though reading my thoughts. "Come. I want to introduce you."

"You know her?"

"Yes, I do. Like you, she's a child of the Most High God."

We walked towards her. Just before we reached her, she turned around. When she saw Michael, she ran up to him, arms open wide. He leaned down to hug her.

"Oh Michael, it's so great to see you!"

I wondered if Michael was also her guardian angel.

"Sarah, I want you to meet Jordan."

A wave of shyness overtook me and I could only respond with a smile.

Michael noticed one of the fishermen struggling with a net. "Looks like he could use some help. Why don't the two of you hang out for a while? I'll be back shortly."

Before I could respond, Michael headed towards the boats, leaving Sarah and me standing alone on the dock.

"So how are you doing, Jordan?" Sarah asked.

I wasn't sure which of me she was referring to, my physical life or my spiritual life. The two had become separate in my mind. "I guess I'm fine."

After a few moments of awkward silence, I said, "I saw you earlier."

"Oh, yeah? Where?"

"You were speaking to a man along the pathway who seemed really upset. Michael called him a standstill."

"Yes, that's true. He is a standstill."

"Do you know him?"

"He's my earthly father." Sarah looked down. I couldn't tell if she was sad or mad.

"Is he upset about something?" I tried to look into her eyes, but she looked away.

"Yes, he is."

"Do you want to talk about it?"

"It's complicated."

"Try me." At this point, I couldn't imagine anything more complicated than my own life.

"I passed away several years ago and my dad is still angry at God about it," Sarah said.

I stared at her in disbelief. "You're dead?" I blurted out. She looked pretty alive to me.

Sarah started laughing. "Oh, Jordan, that's funny. Do I look dead to you?"

"I don't understand, Sarah," I said. At this point, her story did sound more complicated than mine.

"Jordan, physically I died from a rare kind of cancer at the age of seven. My father's a doctor. He thought with all of his knowledge and expertise he could save me, but he couldn't. He's mad at God."

"Why is he mad at God?"

"Because God's will and his will were not the same."

"That must have been hard for him to accept." I wondered in the back of mind if my parents would react the same way if I died. "So God didn't answer his prayers."

Sarah looked deeply into my eyes. "God did answer his prayers, only not in the way he hoped. My father didn't want me to die. Here I am today, alive and stronger than ever." Sarah smiled, looking up at the sky filled with rays of radiant light pouring down from the sky.

"I can understand why it'd hard for your dad."

"Yes. But my real Father is in Heaven. I was a gift given to my parents only for a short period of time," Sarah sighed. "Just seven years."

I stared at her in amazement. I never thought of myself as a gift from God. "But why didn't God save you?"

Sarah laughed. "But God did save me, Jordan. Look at me. Surely you believe in the resurrection."

"Well, yeah. But you're not alive on earth." I wasn't sure where this conversation was going.

"Jordan, do you believe Jesus died for us and three days later was resurrected?"

"Yes, of course."

"And do you believe that all believers receive eternal life through Him?"

"Sarah, I already told you yes! I believe in all of that."

Sarah sat down on the dock and looked out onto the water. I sat down next to her not knowing what to say.

Finally, she broke our silence. "There is a life that leads to death, and a death that leads to life. Do you understand what I'm saying Jordan?"

I remembered Michael saying the same thing just after I had my encounter with the devil, but I wasn't sure I fully understood what it meant.

Sarah picked up some rocks and began throwing them into the water. We watched as they hit the surface, forming circles before sinking to the bottom. "My dad is very sick and time is running out."

"What's wrong with him? Does he have cancer too?"

"What he has is far worse than any cancer or disease. He suffers from spiritual darkness. Cancer attacks the body, but spiritual darkness attacks the soul. Do you know what it means to live in spiritual darkness, Jordan?"

"So, he's not a Christian?"

Tears streamed down her face. "He claims to be Christian. He goes to church and he hears the Message, but that is the extent of it. He never really believed what he said he believed. Do you understand? Do you understand why you're here?"

"Well, yeah. I'm supposed to plant the seed of faith in others in hopes that they will come to know Christ."

"Yes, but hearing the Message is only the beginning. People must also receive it with their hearts, so they will yearn to live according to God's purpose. So many think they live in the light, when actually they live in darkness."

I thought about my own church. How many people attended each Sunday, looking Christian but living in spiritual darkness? And what about those who claimed to be Christian and never went to church? Did they really desire to live life according to God's purpose? Did they even know what God's purpose was?

"Sarah, what if someone believes in Christ but doesn't know God's Will for their lives?"

"A true worshipper of Christ knows in their heart that the will of God is to further His kingdom. We might not fully understand how that happens, especially when bad things happen, but God uses both the good and bad things in life to place people on the pathway to Heaven.

"That's why Michael gave you the seeds, Jordan."

"What about Christians who don't want the same things God wants?" I thought about what happened to me. Sadly I wasn't sure if I wanted what God desired. I thought I was going to play professional sports, now I didn't know if I would live. Cancer was never part of my plan.

"Jordan, Christians are required to fully surrender their lives to Christ, not just the parts they prefer, like Sunday morning. And when bad things happen, we have to trust God knows what He's doing and obey despite the outcome. Each day is not about what we want, but what God wants. And God always wants what's best for our lives."

I took in a deep breath as Sarah's words began to sink in. If what she said was true, then getting cancer was best for my life. I tried to wrap my head around that truth, not knowing if I could.

Sarah looked over at me as if she heard what I was thinking.

"So many Christians believe blessings come from only the good things that happen in our lives. Yet, if bad things never happened, we could easily find ourselves on the pathway to Hell. Do you know which sin can be the most destructive to the soul, Jordan?"

I shrugged my shoulders because I didn't know the answer.

"Complacency," Sarah answered. "Complacency comes from a false sense of security; believing nothing bad will ever happen. We get comfortable and eventually our faith becomes lukewarm. Having lukewarm faith can be very dangerous."

"Why's that?"

"When faith is lukewarm, God becomes an afterthought, except on Sunday mornings. Eventually our hearts turn completely away. We become self-reliant instead of dependent on God. That's what happened to my dad. His success as a doctor overshadowed everything else in his life, including his faith. He had a head knowledge of God, but never a heart knowledge. Do you see?"

"Yeah, I *think* I do." I thought about the people in my life and how so many fell into this same group. Now I understand why my parents, for so many years, took their faith so seriously. Mom wanted to make sure Paige and I understood the importance of God in our lives. At the time, I thought it was annoying, but now I see it differently. My parents never wanted Paige or me to live our lives in spiritual darkness.

"Complacency can be deadly because it attacks the soul, and pretty soon, complacent people begin wandering on the pathway to Hell." Sarah shuddered. "Do you know what life in Hell looks like?"

"I saw the Devil, Sarah. That was frightening enough!"

Sarah looked over my shoulder at a raft tied to the dock. It was made out of tree logs and bounced back and forth as the waves came up to it. "Let's go out into the water. I want to show you something." Sarah grabbed my hand as we stood up and she led me toward the raft.

"Are you sure it's OK? I mean I'm not a great swimmer or anything."

"We'll only go out a few feet. You'll be safe, I promise."

Before I knew it, she was pulling the raft into the water and had gotten on, smiling reassuringly. "Come on!"

When I walked over and stepped onto the raft, Sarah handed me a paddle, then we headed out into the water. Just when we were about twenty feet from the shore, the water instantly turned black around our raft. Sarah took my paddle and laid it on the floor of the raft.

"Sarah, why is the water black?" I began to feel uneasy. Something inside me didn't feel right.

"Look over the edge, Jordan. Look into the water."

I leaned over the edge of the raft and gazed into the water. "I can't see the bottom. The water looks black."

"Keep looking."

As we both stared into the depths, fire appeared under the water.

"What is that? What's happening?" I became terribly frightened. How could a fire be burning under the water?

"Listen."

I could hear moaning, screaming, and the sound of something that reminded me of gnashing of teeth. Just then, hundreds of faces appeared in the water. People's hands were reaching for the surface, as if they wanted me to pull them out. A multitude of bodies burned in the fire—men, women and even children—yet every one of them was alive. Their bodies were scorched with blisters and puss oozed from their wounds. Demons surrounded them, laughing and mocking at their screams. I fell back onto the raft horrified by what I saw. I began feeling nauseated and started to throw up. Tears streamed down my cheeks.

"What's going on?!" I screamed. "What's happening?!"

Tears filled Sarah's eyes. "Those are the ones who heard the message, but their hearts never received it; repentance never happened and their souls became darkened." Sarah was crying. "They chose the pathway to Hell."

"Oh my God, that's awful!" I wanted to get us both out of there quickly! I grabbed my paddle and frantically tried to steer the raft away from the fire and the screaming souls. "Jesus, help us!" I prayed under my breath as we headed towards the shore. Sarah did the same, and the closer we got to land, the lighter the water became. Finally, it returned to crystal blue. My heart was pounding in my chest. I was so winded and overwhelmed by fear, that my shirt was soaked in sweat.

"Are you alright, Jordan?"

I nodded, too shaken to speak.

Once we got to shore, we sat quietly on the raft while I tried to catch my breath.

"I don't know about all this, Sarah." My body trembled all over. "This is too much for me."

"What do you mean? You can make a difference! Plant the seed in others before it's too late."

"Sarah, I'm sick in a hospital bed! Doctors say I'm going to die. I'm only a kid! How does God expect me to save anyone?"

Putting her hand on my shoulder she told me, "You must trust God with all your heart. He knows your circumstances and He will help you. You're not expected to do this alone."

"But what if I fail? I'm just a kid!"

"God never sets His children up for failure. In fact, when we fully turn our lives over to Him, we can only succeed."

"Listen, I prayed for God to help me be all that He needed me to be. But now I wish I hadn't." I knew that sounded awful, but it was the truth. I never wanted cancer. I was scared to be a Kingdom Child.

Sarah smiled as she took my hand and helped me out of the raft. We stepped into the cool water, then pulled the raft up onto the sand. I turned around and looked at the lake. All of the blackness was gone. The water sparkled like diamonds. A cool breeze encircled us, and I smelled roses all around me…yet there weren't any flowers in sight.

"I have a confession to make." Sarah said as she sat down on the grass and looked up into the sky. Her hair shimmered like gold as the light touched her head. "I wasn't thrilled at first about leaving the life I had on earth, but life on earth was the only life I'd seen. Once I saw Jesus, I never wanted to go back."

"What was it like? What was it about Jesus that made you never want to see your family again?"

"I see my family all the time." The corners of her lips turned upward as if attempting a smile, then turned gravely serious. "But the world is filled with evil and darkness. There is no evil or darkness in Jesus. The most wonderful thing about Heaven is everyone is like Jesus. There's no hate, no bitterness, no disease. Only love exists. It's amazing." At that moment, her whole face lit up. She was at peace despite everything that happened to her. I then saw my life and what a mess it was. Cancer had taken over my body. The image of my lifeless body lying in a hospital bed consumed me.

"Why did it have to come to this? Why must my family suffer, seeing me lying helplessly in a coma? This is how I'm to bring others to the kingdom?" As I looked into

Sarah's eyes, they glistened like emeralds, similar to Michael's.

"Jordan, God's purpose is to transform all of us into the likeness of His Son. Often God uses suffering to accomplish His Will. We are called to be Disciples by becoming more like Christ."

"But couldn't God have allowed something less drastic?" My tears returned. Sarah put her arm around my shoulder and handed me the handkerchief she pulled from her pocket. Warmth spread throughout my body as I realized Sarah knew exactly what I was feeling; she'd lived it. Our path's had crossed and our journey's had become one in the same. The look on her face told me she was completely content with her outcome.

"Sarah, I'm sorry," I whispered.

"For what?" she asked sincerely.

"For thinking you wouldn't understand what I'm going through."

Sarah took a deep breath. "As humans, we want to help people avoid suffering, but so often it's our suffering that leads us to Christ."

"But my family already believes."

"Perhaps your suffering is for others, or even for your own faith."

"What do you mean?"

"Our earthly lives are supposed to prepare us for our salvation. Suffering refines us. Trials can actually strengthen our faith and dependence on God. That's why we can be joyful even in our pain."

"Huh?"

"We're supposed to strive daily to become mature and complete Christians. If we're happy all the time and never faced any obstacles, would we even see a need for God?"

"I never would have thought in a million years this would happen to me." I tried to control my emotions, but began to question my faith and whether being a Christian was too hard. "I wish had another calling."

Sarah looked at me curiously. "Another calling? Like what?" She was all ears.

"I don't know. This is too hard! This is too much for me!" Tears flowed freely. I wanted to be strong but I couldn't hold them back any longer. We sat quietly for a while until I could regain my composure.

"What about you, Sarah. Don't you miss your earthly life? Don't you miss going to the mall or hanging out with your friends? You're not angry with God for what happened?"

"Not for a millisecond." Sarah looked up at the sky gleaming.

I looked up to see what she was smiling at, but nothing was there.

"How come? Why don't you miss it? Why aren't you angry?"

"I already told you. I've seen Heaven and I've seen Jesus. Once you've experienced that, you realize there's no other life worth living. All you know is your earthly life. But trust me, you haven't even begun to live until you've experience eternal life firsthand."

"So if God gave you the choice to go back and live an earthly life, would you do it?"

"Why would I go back to a dark and fallen world, where Satan is alive and well, when I can live in the physical presence of Christ in paradise? Once you've experienced Heaven, going back to earth would be painful. I don't know God's plan for you, but if you do have to return, know I will be praying for you."

"Churches don't warn us about evil." I was shaking my head in disbelief. "Michael and I talked about that."

"It's very sad to see churches fail at equipping people for battle," Sarah said. "We think people are the problem, when actually Satan is our problem."

"How's that?"

"Battles aren't against people. They are against the evil forces of the world. Humans are often the vehicles Satan uses to rage wars and destruction. Sadly, many pastors wouldn't recognize the Devil if he hit them over the head. Spiritual warfare is real. You saw it yourself. Don't ever be naïve about that! But believe me, the Holy Spirit is far greater than any of the demonic powers in the world. That's why you don't have to be afraid."

"Michael said that, too."

"Thank God for guardian angels!" Sarah smiled at me as she took in a deep breath. "You know, Jordan, people are saddened when children die, but truthfully, I'm one of the fortunate ones to go early. I don't have to deal with Satan and his evil schemes anymore. I'm free from that."

"I know what you mean. I would rather die than face Satan again." The thought of that made me shudder.

"You're covered in the armor of God, Who never sends us to battle alone. You fight on His strength and not your own. I will pray for you. I will pray that your suffering makes you stronger in Christ."

"But what about your dad? He's in a lot of pain and has turned away from God."

"You only see what's happening on the outside, but God also works on the inside."

"The death of a child is a pretty extreme measure to save a person's soul."

Sarah looked at me intently. By her expression, I knew I'd said something terribly wrong.

"And what about God's plan for salvation? Sacrificing His one and only Son to save mankind was also pretty extreme, don't you think?"

She was right. Jesus gave His life for us, and we are called to be like Him. This was so hard for me to take in. God was asking more of me than I was willing to commit.

"There's no middle ground in the Christian faith, Jordan. You're either all in or not. Are you willing to give up everything, including your life for Him?"

Sarah's words cut deep into my heart. I never understood what it fully meant to be Christian, until now.

"Jordan, before your cancer, you could only see your life from a physical point of view. Now God has given you the gift to see your life and others from a spiritual perspective. In Christ, our lives are not our own. We're all about becoming vessels to be used by God in planting the seed of faith. This is how we further His kingdom."

"But there are *so many* lost souls." I recalled my walk with Michael, witnessing masses of people wandering on the wrong pathways.

"Yes, and perhaps your suffering is what God will use to reach them. Everything happens for a reason. And everything points to the kingdom. Never forget that."

"You know, Sarah, most people have never experienced anything like this; God's Place of Rest, angels and demons. Many will think I'm crazy!" I tried to shake off those remaining images in my head of the lake of fire that still gripped me in fear.

"Yes, maybe so." She looked into the horizon. "And even worse, some of them will be Christians. Satan wants people to be ignorant about his existence and his influence. People only want their pastors to preach all the wonderful things Jesus does for us. But one of the most wonderful things Jesus does is protect us from evil and spiritual warfare. Every day we face a battle. Every day we need a Savior."

"But don't you think if God showed Christians the spiritual world, they would believe in spiritual warfare?"

"Both God and Satan reveal themselves daily. Sadly most Christians don't see with spiritual eyes and aren't able to discern between good and evil. Discernment is a gift from the Holy Spirit. Praise God for this gift He gave you; a picture of both the light and the darkness so that you will never doubt the existence of either."

"I wonder what I will say? How will God use me?"

"The Lord will give you all the words, wisdom, and protection you need. His Spirit will empower you to act with confidence.

Never forget, Jordan, Jesus has already won the battle against Satan, and victory already belongs to every believer."

"OK, I think I'm feeling a little overwhelmed."

"Jordan, we are His Kingdom Children. It's an honor and privilege to serve our Heavenly Father, and the reward is far greater than anything we could ever hope for. Will you do it, Jordan? Will you live out the call to be a Kingdom Child for God? Will you stand with Jesus even if it means giving up the life you once had?"

"Yes. I will certainly try. No one should be left to die in the lake of fire. It was horrible to see so many souls crying out for help! How come you weren't afraid?"

Sarah paused for a moment before responding. "I used to be…but not anymore."

"Are you still afraid of demons?"

"No, Satan doesn't frighten me anymore. Besides, he can't do anything without God's permission. All you have to do is pray. I will also be praying for you."

I wiped my tears onto my shirt and smiled at Sarah. Something told me I would be praying a lot more these days. A voice in the distance called Sarah's name. I looked up and saw a man about a hundred feet away, standing next to a big boat filled with people singing and laughing. It looked like a huge celebration was taking place, and he was inviting her to join them.

Sarah's face lit up. "I'm coming!" She leaped up and turned to hug me. "I love you, Jordan! Thank you! Thank you for everything!"

"For what?" I was confused.

"For doing God's will. Now I know my father will be OK, thanks to your obedience. I had to see it for myself." Sarah's voice was filled with joy.

"How could that be? I don't even know your father."

"Yes, you do. You've already met him. Jim Canon. Dr. Jim Canon. God bless you, Jordan!" Sarah ran down the hill and leaped into the arms of the man who'd called for her. I watched them laugh and hug for quite some time. I wondered if they knew each other from the past.

"Sarah!" I hollered.

She turned around smiling, "Yes, Jordan?"

"Will I ever see you again?"

Sarah and the man both looked at me and started laughing. "Oh, yes! You certainly will!" she yelled back. "I will see you at the feast." She waved to me, and then hopped aboard holding the man's hand. All the people rejoiced at Sarah's arrival. It was like watching a big welcome home party.

Michael appeared by my side.

"Where's she going Michael? Where is the boat taking Sarah and all those people?"

Michael placed his hand on my shoulder. "Home, Jordan. Sarah and the others are finally going to their Heavenly home." We watched the boat fade into a rainbow that covered the mountain top. When I looked at Michael, I noticed we were surrounded by a radiant light pouring down from the sky. But when I looked up, I noticed there wasn't a sun.

Sarah. I was so happy for her. It was like watching someone receive a gift they've waited for their whole life. There was a part of me wishing I was also on that boat, but I knew my work on earth wasn't done.

Michael was sitting on a rock praying. I couldn't understand what he was saying but something told me deep inside he was praying for me.

Chapter Seven

Living in Spiritual Darkness

Dr. Canon's mind was racing as he abruptly left Jordan's room. Was Rosalyn truly waiting for a miraculous sign? Did she really believe God would heal her son? He shook his head in disbelief, pondering their conversation. How could anyone place their trust in an invisible being over the human intellect of leading cancer experts? He once believed in God, but was gravely disappointed after Sarah's death. How many nights did he cry out to God, begging him to heal his daughter, yet nothing happened. It appeared his prayers fell on deaf ears.

Dr. Canon grabbed a cup of coffee and sat alone in the corner of the hospital's cafeteria, watching the workers clean up the tables from the lunch crowd. Rubbing his temples, he reflected back on his religious upbringing as a young boy growing up in a devoted Catholic home. Every room in his house featured a crucifix hanging on a wall, and a statue of Mary was prominently displayed in the front foyer. Each night his mother recited prayers over him and his sister before going to bed. A rosary hung from his bathroom mirror and Mass was attended every Sunday morning. He was taught God was something to fear more than someone to embrace. A Bible wasn't read but revered as the Word of God. He went through the motions of looking religious, but somehow the whole concept of Christianity left him with more questions than answers. Sadly his faith never took root in his life.

Dr. Canon met the love of his life, Annie, while in medical school. Annie was a non-practicing Jew, completing her nursing degree. They married young and decided to put their careers in front of religion. Dr. Canon was making a name for himself as one of the leading surgeons in his city. His success led to a financially comfortable yet hectic lifestyle. Annie decided to retire early and together they wanted to start a family. After several years of trying to conceive, she wasn't able to get pregnant. Every procedure and fertility pill proved unsuccessful. Just before all hope was lost, she finally became pregnant. They found out a baby girl would soon be in their lives, so they named her Sarah.

Grandparents on both sides pressured both Annie and Jim to choose a religious upbringing for their daughter. However, the couple knew whatever they decided, one family would be hurt. Keeping things neutral seemed like the best answer. Sarah would be allowed to choose her own faith when she was older. Growing up, it wasn't uncommon to see both a nativity scene next to a Menorah on their dining room table during the holidays. Ironically, this decision only caused more tension to grow between the families.

Life became busier when Annie went back to work. Dr. Canon's mother stayed with Sarah as the couple tackled a very demanding schedule. During those long days alone with Sarah, Mrs. Canon would share Bible stories and teach Sarah how to pray. Mrs. Canon also had Sarah secretly baptized as a baby without Jim or Annie's knowledge. As she grew older, Sarah loved the songs and stories about Jesus. She asked her parents if she could attend Mass with her grandmother. Reluctantly, they agreed.

When Sarah became ill, her grand-mother would sing Psalms and encourage Sarah to pray every night for Jesus to heal her. One evening, as Dr. Canon was putting her to bed, Sarah shared a prayer that he never forgot. She asked Jesus to take care of her parents. He never understood why she prayed for her parents when it was her life that was in jeopardy.

Night after night, Dr. Canon cried out for God to heal his daughter. The disease had aggressively spread throughout Sarah's body as she became weaker. Then the day came when his own medical team claimed there was nothing more they could do. Days later, his only child passed away. But Sarah wasn't the only one who died, a part of Dr. Canon and Annie died with her. Sarah's death created a void in their marriage that eventually filled itself with anger and hostility. The couple couldn't find comfort or peace within themselves or each other. Eventually their marriage ended and neither one spoke of Sarah again.

Despite his mother's urging of seeking God in his pain, Dr. Canon's heart became filled with resentment. What good was it to believe in a God who allowed a precious young child to die? Dr. Canon had seen so many innocent children die inside the walls of this hospital, causing him to lose all hope in a God of love. And if He did exist, why would He allow so much suffering? Everything in his life had fallen apart, making believing in a loving God an impossible task.

Dr. Canon looked up as the people walked past the cafeteria. He wondered how many of them were parents having to make a life or death decision for their child. He pulled up a picture of his daughter on his cell phone. Sarah's smile lit up her face. Even at her death, she had a peaceful expression. He fought back the tears as memories of her flooded his mind.

His thoughts were interrupted by a ring tone. It was Dr. Mark Andrews, Chief Care Physician over the hospital calling. Rarely did Dr. Canon get a call from his boss.

"Jim, are you free now to stop by my office? I only need ten minutes."

"I'll be right there. Is something wrong?" Dr. Canon asked, but Dr. Andrews had hung up. Jim grabbed a bag of chips and headed to his boss's office. It was going to be one of those days where eating a meal would be a passing thought.

Jim knocked on Dr. Andrews' door. When it opened, he was motioned to come in. Dr. Andrews was on the phone. By his expression, he seemed very concerned about something.

"Thanks for coming on such short notice," he said after hanging up. "It appears we have a problem with one of your patients, Jordan Allen. His parents aren't happy with the level of care being provided and they've asked you be taken off the team."

"I'm aware of how upset they are. Jordan's condition is terminal. No one at our hospital has ever survived this type of tumor. Even if Jordan did, his quality of life could be permanently jeopardized. I don't know how long his parents plan to keep him alive, but every day that goes by, their son is getting weaker. I felt they should know the whole story."

"And you know the whole story?" Dr. Andrews asked, taking his glasses off and looking intently at Jim.

"Of course. Like I said, I've seen this tumor before." Jim responded, agitated by Dr. Andrews questioning of his expertise.

Dr. Andrews stood up and walked around to the front of his desk. "Jim, I know you've had a lot of experience with this kind of cancer and I'm aware of its severity and chances of survival."

"What's your point?"

"What if you are wrong? What if Jordan is an exception?"

"Oh please...you're not suggesting..." Jim stated, shaking his head in disbelief. "I've seen this way too many times! There's no way Jordan can survive this!"

"But there is a way, Jim. Man didn't create the brain so we cannot fully understand the complexity of its natural healing process."

Jim looked into Dr. Andrews eyes, trying to stay calm, then took a deep breath. "What are you suggesting?"

"That you be patient with the Allen's. When there's breath, there's hope. We must do all we can and see if Jordan can beat the odds."

"I think you're making a mistake."

"Maybe. But I do believe his parents will know what to do in time regarding their son." Dr. Andrews sat down and turned his focus to his computer, a sign their conversation was over. Jim moved to the doorway and stared at Dr. Andrews back.

"How long will you allow this?"

"What's your point Jim?" Dr. Andrews replied, still facing his computer.

"Will you stand behind the ethics committee if they agree with my assessment, or will you stand with the parents? Which side are you on?"

Dr. Andrews turned around and looked at Jim, massaging the back of his neck before finally speaking. "Jim, you've already given up. You've delayed treatment. You've written off his life before even trying to save it. You of all people should be sensitive to this issue. Now that's all I have to say about it." Dr. Andrew's phone rang, and he ceremoniously motioned Jim to leave.

As Jim walked out into the hospital corridor, he thought about Dr. Andrew's comment. *It's not that I want Jordan to die. I just don't want to create any false hope by prolonging his suffering. Could I be wrong? Have I written off the life of a young boy too soon? Would Jordan be another statistic, or would a miraculous event save him?*

Jim believed what made him a good doctor was that he could remove all emotions when having to make life or death decisions for patients and their families. *Maybe the heart shouldn't be removed in a decision like this. Maybe the heart and mind are supposed to work together. But that would go against all of my medical intellect. Have I hardened my heart to the point of becoming a skeptic of divine intervention?*

He took a deep breath, trying to shake off the confusing thoughts. At the end of the hall, he found a chair and sat for a moment, pondering what he should do. *Maybe Andrews has a point.* As nurses and doctors brushed past him, he felt so removed from his environment.

Memories flooded his mind of the final days he had with his daughter in the hospital. It was so painful to see someone he loved die from a disease he couldn't stop. He begged God to save his daughter. He pleaded for a miracle, but lost her anyway. *After witnessing that, I couldn't possibly believe in something that leads to such sadness and disappointment.*

As Dr. Canon stared at the floor, trying to regain his composure, two angels sent by Jesus appeared and prayed over him.

***

Jordan's Story

From the lakeside where Michael and I were standing, Sarah's boat could no longer be seen.

"Come, let's go get you something to eat," Michael said.

I eagerly agreed. I loved the food in God's Place of Rest and my appetite had increased since I got here. Michael and I walked a little ways before coming upon a picnic table with a basket filled with cheeses, fresh fruit, and miniature chocolate cakes. "Wow, look at that! Is that for us, Michael?" I couldn't wait to eat.

"Yes, help yourself." We sat down and I took a pear from the basket. There wasn't one flaw on its skin and the shape was perfect, without any indentation. Before taking a bite, I noticed Michael smiling at me. He was waiting on me to give thanks to God before eating.

I bowed my head and began praying. "Heavenly Father, thank You for all that You're showing me. Thank You for Sarah. Thank you for Michael. Help me to brave. Help me to be all You need me to be. Amen." I said it; the prayer that led me to this point in my life. Earlier, I had confessed to Sarah I didn't know if I wanted what God wanted. Everything had become so complicated. But I had to trust God and believe He knew what He was doing. *Help me to trust You. Help me to believe in You*, I said silently to myself. I thought of my parents and how hard this was on them. I thought about Paige and how she was handling everything. When I opened my eyes, the light from above shone all around us. I felt like I was sitting in the middle of a rainbow.

"Michael, do you know Sarah's story?"

"Yes, I know it well."

"Do you know everyone's story in God's Place of Rest?"

"Yes, Jordan, I do. And some day you will see how all the stories fit together."

"But how's that possible?"

"The journey of every Christian points to the same destination. And every person who comes across your path is no coincidence." Michael looked at the majestic mountain where Heaven was. No matter where I was in God's Place of Rest, I could always see that mountain. Its base was encircled with radiant lights and the top sparkled like diamonds. I'd never seen anything more beautiful. When Michael turned to look at me, his face was radiant like the sun. For a moment I had to close my eyes because of its brightness.

"Michael, you're glowing," I said, squinting my eyes.

Michael smiled and took a piece of fruit. After a few moments, his complexion became normal.

"What caused your face to look like that?"

"The glory of God," Michael responded.

"Will my face glow one day?"

"Yes, it sure will. When your physical body dies, your sinful nature also dies. One day, you will be like Jesus, completely free of sin and filled with God's glory."

"I can't imagine that." I looked down, trying to hold back my tears, remembering myself lying in a hospital bed with tubes and machines connected to my body.

Michael looked at me with such compassion and placed his arm around me. We sat quietly for a while.

"Here, try one of these." Michael handed me a piece of chocolate. As I bit into it, the sweetness of coco filled my mouth. I looked at the chocolate more closely because this was quite different than what I've eaten before. The chocolate was actually warm on the inside, similar to a pudding.

"Wow, that's really good." I took another bite while thinking about all that's happened. I was wondering how Sarah was doing as I recalled our conversations.

"Sarah showed me the lake of fire, Michael. I'd never seen anything so horrible!" I was still shaken from that event.

"Yes, it's tragic for anyone to spend even a second of time there."

"So how does someone end up there, Michael?"

"Anyone whose name is not written in the Book of Life will go there."

"The Book of Life?"

"Yes. This Book has every name of God's children written in it. And these people will all receive the gift of salvation through Jesus Christ."

"So the really bad people aren't included?"

"What is your definition of a really bad person, Jordan?"

"You know, people who do really bad things, like murderers."

"Jordan, you have the same sinful nature as a murderer. You're just as capable of killing someone as anyone else. Did you know many of the saints written about in the Bible murdered innocent lives? Surely you've heard of Moses or David, the king of Israel? And there are others as well."

"Oh, yeah. I guess you're right. So I guess we are all really bad people."

"Yes, that's true. But every person, good and bad, has an opportunity to make things right with God through faith in His Son. There's not one sin that can't be forgiven. However, life without repentance leads to death."

"I never realized how important repentance was."

"Repentance is what leads to the transformation of every Christian."

"How do you know if your life has been transformed?"

"Look at your own life. How is it different?"

"Physically, I'm in a coma fighting for my life." Just hearing that was so surreal to me, especially since I felt so alive in God's Place of Rest.

"What about spiritually? What's changed about you and your faith?" Michael asked, reaching for a piece of chocolate.

I thought about Michael's question. My faith certainly had changed. Being a Christian came with responsibility. It's not about living a "happily ever after" life. It's about facing tough times with faith and believing God will get you through it. It's about furthering God's kingdom no matter what the cost. Before cancer, none of this seemed important to me. But I had changed. Things were now very different spiritually.

"What matters to me now are the same things that matter to God," I answered. "And I never really thought about sin being a big deal. But Christians are called to be different. It's a life or death decision. I see that now."

"God has always set His children apart from the rest of the world. Remember, Jordan, you are in the world, but you're not of the world. You've been made new."

I smiled at Michael thinking about what he said. I had changed, not only physically but even more so spiritually. Faith had become so real whereas before, it was something I only thought about on Sunday morning. Never before did I give much thought to those who aren't Christians and what that meant for their eternity. I certainly never thought much about Hell or the Devil. But now my eyes were opened. I could both see and feel about things from a divine perspective. My heart desired to help people find the pathway to the Heavenly Mountain. Being a Christian was more than a religion. It was a responsibility to be all that God calls us to be.

"I'm so sorry, God." I began to cry. I couldn't stop. I hoped my tears would wash away all the guilt stored inside my heart. "I told Sarah this was too hard. I'm not worthy of being a Kingdom Child."

"Oh, but you are, Jordan, and even more so today! The fact that you recognize your calling is what makes you a Kingdom Child." Michael removed my hands from my face and placed his hands on my cheeks, looking deeply into my eyes. I felt a breath of inner strength filling every pore in my body. I looked down at my palms and noticed they had tiny little sparkles on them.

"Look, Michael! Look at my hands!"

Michael smiled. "If anyone is in Christ, he is a new creation; the old has gone, the new has come!" (2Corinthians 5:17).

Instantly, my sadness vanished. An inexpressible feeling of pure joy bubbled up inside of me.

"I can't wait to tell everyone what's happened! I can't wait to tell everyone about Jesus!"

Michael hugged me. "Jordan, come with me. I want to show you something."

We headed down a hill towards the people wandering along the pathways. As we passed by, no one seemed to notice us. Those who did look our way appeared to have the weight of the world upon their shoulders. Their bodies slumped over and their facial expressions looked drawn and worn down by life. They wandered aimlessly from pathway to pathway, many headed in the opposite direction of Heaven.

"Michael, why won't these people even look at me?" I tried smiling at some but they looked right passed me; only a few ever made eye contact. One person walked by and glanced my way. "Wait! Hey that person goes to my church, and that one is a teacher from my school!" I noticed they were on the wrong pathway. "They're Christians, right?"

"They're church attendees. But just attending church doesn't make someone Christian."

As I looked closer, I stopped right in my tracks startled by who I saw walking on the wrong pathway.

"Oh my gosh, Michael! Do you know who that is? That's one of the pastors at my church! He's on the wrong pathway!"

Michael turned and let out a big sigh. "Even pastors can live in spiritual darkness."

"But how can that be?" I asked, bewildered. I ran up to him to see if he would recognize me, but he didn't. My pastor walked right past me as though we were complete strangers.

"How can he not know who I am?"

"Because you're not who you think you are. You are a new creation."

"What do you mean?"

"You've been born again by God's Holy Spirit. Everything in your physical world will be different because you will see things from a Heavenly perspective. Christians who haven't undergone this kind of transformation won't recognize the person you've become, or understand what's happened. Michael looked at the pastor. "His soul doesn't recognize yours because he's never been transformed."

"But he's a pastor! He's been to seminary school and must have a hundred degrees hanging on the wall in his office!"

"And all of his intellect and training will never lead him to God. Remember the disciples? None of them were scholars, yet they were all divinely changed. It was their heart, not their head that made their faith authentic."

"I never thought that could happen to a pastor." I watched as he wandered down the wrong pathway.

"It can happen to anyone, even pastors."

I thought back to my conversation with him about the devil.

"You know, Michael, he doesn't believe in Satan."

"Yes, I know. What's even worse is he thinks he's on the pathway to Heaven."

"So if God gives me the chance to tell him all I've seen, he'd probably think I was crazy!"

"Well, at least you'd be in good company. At one point, even Jesus' own mother thought He had lost His mind. Jesus was both human and God in one. He had one foot in the physical world while the other foot was in the spiritual world. That's why He could see both angels and demons. You also have one foot in the physical and one foot in the spiritual world. Remember you're in the world, but you're not of it."

"What will happen to my pastor? Will he ever find his way back to the right path?"

"There's always hope for a person's eyes to be opened."

"What can I do to help?"

"Pray for the scales to be removed from his eyes. Pray for his heart to be enlightened by every message written in the Bible, not just the one's he chooses to believe. Pray for his repentance that can lead to divine change."

"What does that look like? Am I able to see a repented soul?"

"You most certainly are. Come with me."

In an instant, we were in another part of God's Place of Rest I'd never seen. The people were different than those I previously saw on the pathways. No one looked lost or wandered aimlessly. Yet by the clothes they were wearing, many appeared poor. Some of the children were so thin I thought they would break in two. As they picked berries and gathered food for their baskets, pure joy filled their hearts as they sang songs in the fields. Unlike others I had seen, no one looked depressed or appeared angry. Some were dancing and praising God with their hands lifted to the sky.

"What are those shacks used for?" I pointed to structures made out of mud and sticks. I wondered if a strong wind could blow them down in an instant.

"Those are the homes for these families." Michael smiled while watching the people sing and dance. As we walked by, many smiled and waved at us. Several spoke, but I didn't understand their language.

"What are they saying?"

"Some are saying, 'God bless you,' while others are saying 'God is good,'" Michael replied.

"How can they be so happy when they're so poor? Do they even have enough food and water?"

"They trust God will provide for all their needs," Michael said. "Look at their spirits; look beyond their physical state and see what God sees."

I stared for quite some time. Their smiles lit up their whole faces. "Joy. I see pure joy." *How could anyone be so joyful with so little?*

"The Bible says, 'Seek His kingdom first and His righteousness and your needs will be met.' (Matthew 6:31-34). The problem is many of us have confused wants with needs. To you they seem poor and deprived, but to God, they are rich and their treasures are stored in Heaven. They don't live for the things of this world. They live for eternity.That joy you see can only come from the Holy Spirit. Their faith is continuous and steadfast both in good and bad times."

"So they never get depressed?"

"Of course they do; they're human. But they know trials develop perseverance and perseverance is what strengthens their faith. These people have little-to-no education, yet they know more about God than most living in your affluent community, including your pastor."

Seeing their lives made me realize what was lacking in mine. I had food at my fingertips, and all the toys and gadgets I could possibly want, yet none of it brought me the kind of joy these people were experiencing. As a teenager living in a nice neighborhood, I thought I had it all. But in that moment, I realized how little I truly had.

"Jordan, God has blessed you with the desires of your heart. But sometimes the gifts we receive become stumbling blocks in our relationship with Him. People desire the gifts, but not always the Giver. People want to be blessed, but not if it means becoming divinely changed."

As I watched the people around me, I felt empty inside. Maybe God has blessed me too much. "I guess I've been living too comfortable."

"Only if your level of comfort causes you to become complacent. Complacency can lead to spiritual death."

"I always thought people in other countries were in need of God, but now it's clear many in my own neighborhood are spiritually dead. What can I do to help?"

"You must return to your physical state."

"But I'm in a coma. I can't talk to people."

"Maybe it's not your voice others need to hear. Trust God. He knows what He's doing." Michael smiled while hugging me.

"Sarah thinks I can help her dad."

"What do you think? Are you willing to help Sarah's dad and maybe others as well? Are you willing to trust and obey God no matter what the outcome?"

"I want to, Michael. I just don't see how it's going to work."

"We can only see the present, but God sees our past, present, and future. Take it one day at a time."

"So what happens now?"

"It's time for you to return to your earthly body."

"I don't understand."

"Your body, soul, and spirit will become one again. But before you leave God's Place of Rest, let's pray."

We sat down on the ground and held hands. A part of me was scared to go back to the hospital. I didn't know what I would face, but I had to trust God. I had to believe He knew what He was doing. Michael took in a deep breath while I waited to hear what he would pray. "Heavenly Father, how wondrous You are. Your love is deeper than the oceans. We come before You eager to do Your will. Please give Jordan Your courage and Your

strength so that he may accomplish Your
purpose. Remind him that the power in Your
name will overcome any darkness he faces.
Help him to never waver from Your path of
righteousness. Oh gracious God, we thank
You for allowing us this opportunity to serve
You. In Jesus' name we pray, amen."

I opened my eyes. Michael was
smiling at me.

"Are you ready, Jordan?"

"What's going to happen now?"

"It's time to go to work. Now close
your eyes."

As I closed my eyes, I felt a warm
breath of air encircle me, covering me like a
warm blanket, then I became sleepy. I could
feel my body being lifted in the air. Michael
held my hand while whispering something,
but I couldn't understand what he was saying.

"Michael?" I couldn't open my eyes.

"Don't worry, God is always with
you. Remember, your struggle isn't against
flesh and blood but against the powers of this
dark and fallen world. Jesus will always
protect you. He will fight your battles. Just
believe in Him."

When I finally could open my eyes, I
was in a dark room. I had returned to the
hospital.

I didn't know for sure if I was
dreaming or if I was awake. My body was
chilled from head to toe.

"Jordan," a voice spoke from the corner of the room. I looked, but couldn't see anyone. However, this voice was familiar. It was the voice of Satan. "Jordan, surely you know God has sent you back here to die."

I tried to scream, but nothing came out of my mouth.

"Jordan, you don't really believe you can save others. You're just a child dying from cancer in a hospital."

Then I saw the shadow in the corner of the room, and it started walking towards me.

"Jordan, let's end this nonsense right now. Let's end this suffering," Satan said. "Give me your soul and I will heal you immediately."

Michael told me not to listen to him; to call on the name of Jesus. In the name of Jesus Christ, get out! I shouted in my head. *Protect me, Jesus!*

In an instant the enemy vanished. I closed my eyes, whispering the Lord's Prayer to myself. I could hear my parent's voices talking softly in the room, but didn't know what they were saying. I felt another presence in the room, but this time I was comforted. Jesus was sitting on my bed. I couldn't see Him but I knew in my heart He was with me. I tried to lift up my hand to touch Him. Jesus took my hand and placed it on my heart. He placed His other hand on my head and I felt a warm sensation come over me as He blessed me. I knew as long as He was with me, I would be safe from the enemy's presence. I tried to whisper thank you but couldn't form the words. Yet in my heart I heard Him say, "You're mine."

Chapter Eight

The Awakening

Rosalyn's Story

Sam and I sat quietly in the hospital room watching TV, while waiting for any sign of life from Jordan. He was still in a coma and only God knew if he would ever wake up. I missed hearing his voice. While he slept, I often played his voice message on his cell phone just so I could hear the sound of him speaking. It brought us hope of one day hearing him speak again and hopefully having a full recovery.

While sitting quietly next to his bedside, there was a knock on our door. A woman entered and introduced herself as someone from the palliative care team.

"Mr. and Mrs. Allen, my name is Donna Jacobs. How's Jordan doing today?"

Sam stood up to greet her. "Jordan is doing fine."

"That's good to hear. How are both of you doing?"

"We're hanging in there, Ms. Jacobs," Sam responded cordially.

"I wanted to come by and introduce myself. Our team is here to keep Jordan comfortable."

"Well, we're a long way off from having a conversation with your department," Sam replied. I remained quiet, trying to keep my emotions intact.

"Yes, of course. Perhaps at some point, we may need to discuss your plans for end of life."

I couldn't keep quiet any longer, interrupting Sam before he could speak. "Ms. Jacobs, we won't be having that discussion with you. God will have the final say. And when we hear from God, we will let you know. Why does everyone seem to be waiting for Jordan to die when maybe it's God's plan for him to live? He brought him back once. Maybe He'll do it again."

Sam placed his arm around me, a subtle way of quieting me.

"Of course, Mrs. Allen. We only want the best for you and your son."

"If that were true, treatment would have started immediately," Sam jumped in. "Who's responsible for sending people like you to tell us what's best for Jordan?" He sat down, trying to calm his voice.

"Mr. Allen, I know this is difficult."

"I'm tired of everyone giving up so quickly. It's only been seven days and all you want us to do is quit! Why can't you have just a little faith? Why won't you at least try to save our son? Let's try chemo! Let's try radiation! Let's try something!" I was screaming at the top of my lungs. "Why can't you wait a little longer for God to respond! Why can't—"

A small voice was heard coming from Jordan's bed. "Mama."

One simple word from Jordan's mouth changed everything. I looked over at our son and noticed his eyes were opened.

"Oh my God, Jordan!" I cried out, reaching for his hand.

Sam rushed to his side. "Jordan, can you hear me?"

Ms. Jacob's face was white as a ghost as she stood speechless in the doorway staring at Jordan. She grabbed the monitor and pressed the button. Several nurses raced into our room as Jordan woke up from his coma.

"Oh my God! Get a doctor!" One nurse ran out while the other checked his vital signs.

I couldn't believe it! It seemed like eternity since I had heard his voice.

"Jordan, it's Mommy. Baby, if you can hear me, squeeze my hand."

I felt a gentle squeeze. Tears began streaming down my cheeks as I praised God for giving us another miracle!

Meanwhile, the nurse found Dr. Canon and told him what happened.

***

Jordan's Story

As I looked into my mother's eyes, I tried to speak but wasn't able to form words with my mouth. Desperately I wanted to say something, but I could barely move my lips. Exhaustion came over me. My body was so cold, yet I could feel the warmth of Mom's hand holding mine. I noticed several machines by my bedside monitoring my vital signs. Reality hit me—I was no longer strong and healthy like I was in God's Place of Rest. I was lying in a hospital bed suffering from a brain tumor. My heart was pounding inside my chest. The right side of my body felt tingly. I tried to move my fingers, but couldn't lift my right hand. *What's happening?* A thousand questions were racing through my mind.

A doctor appeared at my bedside. My mother stepped aside, giving him more room. He leaned over and looked closely in my eyes, shining a bright light into my pupils.

"Jordan, can you hear me?" the doctor asked.

I looked into the doctor's eyes but couldn't respond. I tried to focus on his name tag—Dr. Canon. *Why's his name familiar?*

"Jordan, I'm Dr. Canon. Squeeze my hand if you can hear me."

My right hand felt like it was no longer attached to my body. Trying to hold back my tears, I was overwhelmed as every emotion overtook me. I was happy to see my parents, yet devastated by my physical condition. I was happy to be alive, yet fearful of my diagnosis. I tried to speak again, but couldn't move my lips.

"Take your time, Jordan. Think about what you're doing."

Dr. Canon's voice was calming to my spirit. As I looked into his eyes, I recalled my conversation with Sarah just before she got on the boat. She was thanking me for helping her father. Dr. Canon was his name. Was this man her father?

"Dr. Canon, he can use his left hand." I heard Mom's voice. Dr. Canon reached for my left hand. With every ounce of energy I had, I squeezed his fingers. He smiled at me as he whispered quietly, "My God, how can this be?"

Dr. Canon turned to one of the nurses. "We'll start chemo and radiation imme-diately. Jordan, we're going to put a port in you. That way we don't have to poke your arms with needles. Welcome back, son. We're glad you're with us." Dr. Canon smiled as I slowly lifted my hand to show a 'thumbs up.'

I wondered how God was going to use me to help this man. I truly was at God's mercy. I had to trust Him to show me what to do since I felt helpless.

Mom was crying tears of joy. It was wonderful to see her praising God in the midst of this. Dad was on the phone with my uncle giving him an update on my condition.

A nurse wheeled my bed out of the room and we headed down the hospital corridor. I noticed a man standing in the hallway, observing everything that was happening. His hair was long and gray, pulled back into a ponytail. He wore a denim shirt with blue jeans. He looked at me and smiled as I wheeled passed him. His eyes sparkled like emeralds and his face was vaguely familiar. *Where have I seen him before?* I closed my eyes, trying to remember everything that happened. *When was I admitted? Would I return to God's Place of Rest, or was it a dream?* It seemed I was living in two different worlds; the physical and the spiritual. And both of them had just collided.

***

Rosalyn's Story

After seven long days, treatment for Jordan finally began. Chemo injections, radiation, and various antibiotics were poured into his body. Doctors remained puzzled over the turn of events. Our son was finally receiving medical treatment and this brought a sense of relief to both me and Sam. Something was being done to try and save Jordan.

This was the second time the Lord brought Jordan back to life. We recognized God's divine intervention, but didn't know if the doctors could see it the same way. God could have taken Jordan, but He didn't. There was a reason Jordan remained with us. Meanwhile, we praised God for more time with our son, knowing the Great Physician would always have the final say.

***

Jordan's Story

As I was wheeled into the operating room, I tried opening my eyes to see what was happening.

"Jordan, we're going to give you a little something to help you sleep. When you

wake up, we'll visit again." Dr. Canon smiled
as he reached over to squeeze my hand.

Mom once told me a person's eyes are
the windows into their soul. Physically, Dr.
Canon was a handsome man with dark-brown
eyes, probably in his mid-forties. But behind
his physical appearance, his eyes revealed a
grieving soul. I wanted to cry out Sarah's
name and assure him she was alive and well. I
wanted to tell him Heaven was a real place.

"Sar, s, s." I tried to say her name, but
wasn't able to form words. My eyes became
heavy as I fell into a deep sleep.

"It's OK, Jordan. We'll talk soon, I
promise." Dr. Canon stood quietly over
Jordan as his thoughts returned to Sarah and
the many sleepless nights by her bedside in a
cold dark hospital room. How many nights
did he kneel at the foot of her bed, pleading
for God to take his life instead. Dr. Canon
closed his eyes, trying to suppress the pain
that left his heart empty and darkened.

"Are you ready, Doctor?" A nurse
interrupted his thoughts.

Dr. Canon nodded as he began
inserting the port into Jordan's chest.

My spirit stood outside my body and
watched the procedure from across the room
as the walls of the hospital opened up. My
jaw dropped while standing in God's Place of
Rest. I turned around looking for Dr. Canon
and the medical team, but they were gone. I

glanced towards the lake and saw Michael fishing along the shore. He turned and waved as I ran into his arms, relieved to be with him again.

"Michael, what's happening? Am I dreaming?"

"Your body is sleeping. Michael picked up a fishing pole and began stringing a worm on its hook. "Here you go. It's time for you to become a fisherman."

I took the fishing pole and cast my line into the water.

"Now comes the hard part, Jordan— waiting." Michael smiled as we sat on some rocks along the shoreline. The waves rocked our bobbers back and forth, creating an illusion of fish tugging on our lines. The water glistened like diamonds as rays of light bounced on its surface. I looked up into the sky, but couldn't see the light's source.

"Michael, where does the light come from? I don't see the sun."

"That's because there isn't a sun in God's Place of Rest. There's no need for it. The light you see is the glory of God."

I stood in amazement as I observed the light as it stretched from east to west. This particular light looked different from sun rays, everything it touched came alive. The branches of trees stretched towards it as if wanting each leaf to embrace its light. The flowers seemed to be smiling as the colors of their petals sparkled like jewels. To stand in its presence was overwhelming. Even the blades of grass stretched towards the light, capturing its warmth. The animals looked into the light as though acknowledging God's presence around them. I reached out to touch one of the rays with my fingers. Instantly, I felt an inner strength as everything inside me came alive. "Wow!" I stood in amazement. "So that's God!"

"The light is a facet of God's glory and a reflection of His presence. Christ is the Light of the World, and His light brings life into everything that receives it."

"Why don't I feel this in the physical world?"

"You certainly can, but often the distractions of the world hinder us from experiencing the fullness of His presence."

I closed my eyes, taking in every moment of God's glory as it rested on me like a warm, soft blanket. I closed my eyes, envisioning God holding my face in the palms of His hands. "I wish everyone could experience this."

"They can. Seek and you shall find."

"Can I feel this in a cold dark hospital with tubes coming out of my body?"

"When we face trials with faith, that's when we can experience it the most."

"Michael, how do people deal with suffering without God? I've seen so much and

I know Heaven is real. But what about people who don't believe in God or Heaven? Where do they turn for help or comfort?"

Michael bowed his head and hugged me close. "I don't know. I truly don't know."

"What about Dr. Canon? What does he do to get through his pain?" My stomach hurt as the image of his grieving soul ran through my mind.

"Sadly, he suppresses his pain by pushing it deep down inside," Michael said with a long sigh. "So often we seek comfort from other sources, but this can leave us feeling even more discouraged."

"He once believed in God, didn't he Michael?"

"His faith was never grounded. The seed planted never took root. God has His reasons for allowing trails. We have to trust Him, no matter what the outcome."

"You keep telling me that," I replied smiling.

"Well, obviously it bears repeating," Michael responded joyfully.

"Dr. Canon is Sarah's dad, right?"

"Yes, that's correct."

Just then, I remembered a man in the hospital corridor with long white hair as I wheeled passed him. "Michael, you were that man standing in the hallway!"

"Yes, I was him." Michael said smiling.

"Wow, I can see angels even on earth! How awesome is that!"

"God reveals His angels all the time. But one's faith must be deeper than a weekly church service in order to see them."

"I tried to speak to Dr. Canon, but couldn't. How can I tell him about Sarah if I can't talk?"

"Sometimes our words get in the way of doing God's work. Maybe for now, just be silent and wait for God."

"But wouldn't it would be easier if I could tell Dr. Canon with my own words that I met Sarah?"

Michael hugged me. "Yes, Jordan, I suppose that would be easier. But more often than not, it's our actions and not our words that bring others to Christ. Sarah's dad is angry at God for allowing Sarah to die. Yet what we can't see is the depth of God's work in a person, especially when it comes to dealing with the death of a loved one."

"So how will God use me to help Sarah's dad?"

Michael laughed. "Well, here's what I do know. God has a plan; just be patient and wait. Today you are fisherman, but in days ahead, you will become a fisher of men."

I turned my attention to the bobber bouncing on the water's surface, wondering if I would ever catch a fish. I took in a deep sigh before noticing Michael sitting, yet his arms were in a constant motion as he cast his line into deeper water. He never seemed tired or impatient. Perhaps I needed to follow his example. Rather than sitting back and waiting for the fish to come to me, I needed to actively pursue them.

"Michael, does God ever take a vacation?"

Michael burst into laughter. "Jordan, pray that God never takes one second of vacation. I would hate to think how worse off the world would be if He did."

"This won't be easy."

"Being a Kingdom Child was never meant to be easy; it was meant to be fruitful. There may be times when giving up seems like the only option, but have faith in God. He's planning each step along your journey. You're not in this alone."

I was relieved knowing God didn't expect me to do this on my own. I needed God, and even if I couldn't see Him, knowing He was there gave me encouragement. I didn't want to fight cancer alone. I didn't want to fight the Devil alone. And knowing God would have the final say, gave me tremendous peace.

As I thought about the spiritual world and the physical world, I was beginning to see how these two worlds aren't separate, but are intertwined into one. Things that happen in the physical world impact the spiritual. And things that happen spiritually, impact the physical. Cancer, the culprit of my physical world, wasn't pointing to the end, but to a new beginning with a divine purpose.

I looked over at Michael and noticed him smiling at me as though reading my thoughts. As he reached for my hand, I felt a tingling sensation in my right arm. This arm had lost all feeling in the hospital. Yet in God's Place of Rest, it was completely healed.

"What's happening to my body physically? I know I have a brain tumor, but how will it affect me?" I wasn't sure if I wanted to hear the answer to my question.

"For a while, you will have limited mobility. The things humans take for granted such as eating, drinking, walking, and even breathing will be difficult for you, if not impossible. But this is all part of God's plan. People will be drawn into your family's life as waves are drawn to the seashore. The faith of your family will become like a magnet to some. Many will be moved by your parent's courage and strength."

"Are any of these people standstills or nonbelievers?"

"Yes. That's exactly who I'm talking about. People who never prayed before will fall to their knees after meeting your family. And that's just the beginning of how God will use you to further His kingdom. But not everyone will receive your family's faith."

"What do you mean?"

"Some will fall away. Your parents' testimony may lead others into spiritual darkness. Some won't understand your mother's joy in the Lord, while her son is suffering from a brain tumor. And others will think your parents have gone off the deep end for fighting to keep you alive."

"So, why do some of the doctors want to end my life?"

Michael paused a long time before answering my question. He looked up into the sky as if waiting for God to respond to my question.

"It's not that they want to end your life. They don't want to prolong your suffering or your family's."

"Does Dr. Canon want me to die?"

"Jordan, Dr. Canon doesn't want you to die, yet he knows he can't save you, just like he couldn't save Sarah."

"So ending my life sooner would make it easier for my family? Is that what he believes?"

Michael wrapped his arms around me and held me close. I took in a deep breath while feeling my angel's arms embrace me.

"God will have the final say, right?" I asked, burying my face into Michael's shirt.

"God always has the final say," Michael said with conviction.

"Does Dr. Canon pray?"

"Not since Sarah's death. He's lost his way and it's our job to help lead him back to the right pathway."

"But what if I die Michael? Then Dr. Canon was right."

"Do you think that's what this is all about? Proving who is right and who is wrong? The only thing Dr. Canon is right about is his inability to save human lives. God is always right and only He can save you."

"But how could Dr. Canon believe in God after Sarah's death? God didn't save Sarah and that broke his heart."

"Are we only to believe in God when things go our way, Jordan?"

As I looked closer, I spotted Dr. Canon standing alone on the pathway leading to Hell. I shook my head in disbelief.

"God would help Dr. Canon, right?"

"Of course, He would, but the ball is in Dr. Canon's court. God will never force Himself upon anyone. When we come to God with a humble heart, that's when repentance begins and lives become divinely changed. Keep praying for him. Nothing is impossible with God."

At that moment, I began to fade away from Michael's presence. I closed my eyes, feeling my spirit depart from God's Place of

Rest. When I opened them, I was back in the hospital. My body and spirit had become one.

Chapter Nine

Accepting God's Plan

Jordan's Story

God's Place of Rest seemed like a fantasy after returning to my physical condition. God hadn't healed me, and truthfully, I wasn't sure if He would. My world had turned upside down. Things were different both physically and spiritually. Physically I was weak, battling a fatal brain tumor and relying on machines to help with simple tasks such as breathing and eating. Each day I didn't know if I would live or die. I closed my eyes trying to recall my life before cancer. Playing football, basketball, and hanging out with friends were memories from a distant past. My family was the only reason for wanting to remain in this world.

Spiritually, I was a new person. In God's Place of Rest, I was strong and healed both inside and out. Not one bruise or scar touched my skin. Before my illness, I never put a lot thought into how my faith was to be

used to further God's kingdom. I knew I was
going to Heaven and that seemed sufficient.
But being a Christian isn't supposed to be
about me, but about God using me to show
others the right pathway. Images of the
standstills filled my mind as I envisioned their
souls wandering towards Hell. These were the
ones claiming to be Christian, but only
knowing Jesus by name. They were as lost as
the nonbelievers. I never realized so many
people were dying spiritually and didn't even
know it. Truthfully there was a part of me
who wanted to leave the physical world and
forget about all of these hurting people. But
God had a reason for keeping me alive. The
seed of faith needed to be planted. Lives
needed to be divinely changed, and that is the
calling of a Kingdom Child.

While lying in my hospital bed, I
noticed there wasn't a tube in my mouth. I
was breathing through a mask strapped
around my nose. I lifted my hand, trying to
grab the bed rail. Mom immediately came to
my side.

"Hi, sweetie. How are you doing?"

I could only look at her, hoping she
could see my heart smiling.

"Can you squeeze my hand, Jordan?"

Her hand felt warm as it cupped mine.
With all my strength, I tried to squeeze her
fingers. She smiled and kissed my forehead.
Just then, a nurse entered our room.

"Hey Jordan," the nurse said smiling. "How are you doing?"

I gave her a 'thumbs up.'

"I thought we might like a sponge bath today," she said, looking at Mom.

"Sure, that would be great," Mom said, most appreciatively.

I had to get over the fact that nurses saw naked bodies every day. It must be a "mom thing" to care about my hygiene, and Mom seemed happy knowing I was clean. When the nurse finally finished, I felt better. I didn't feel humiliated anymore. Mom kissed me on the forehead then spoke privately with the nurse.

I stared at the ceiling trying not to feel sorry for myself, but cancer was a joy killer. The longer I was awake, the more sensitive I became of my condition. I thought about Paige and how this was affecting her. I was her big brother, her shield of protection, but I couldn't protect her now. I closed my eyes reflecting on Michael's words: "Trust God no matter what."

Quietly, I said a prayer to myself.

Dear God, help me to have faith larger than a mustard seed.

I quickly fell into a deep sleep, but this time I didn't return to God's Place of Rest. I was standing in the middle of a large angry crowd of people screaming, "Crucify Him!"

Where am I? Am I dreaming? I turned to look in the crowd's direction and gasped at what I saw! It was Jesus hanging on a cross! Blood was pouring from His hands and feet where the nails were driven in. His flesh was ripped from head to toe and His face was severely bruised and disfigured. I felt faint as the crowd yelled out, "Look at the King of the Jews now!"

Filled with despair, I fell to the ground. The wind was knocked out of me as my body pressed against others. *Wake Up! Wake Up!* I said to myself, but I couldn't. *Why am I here? Why did God want me to see this?* I grabbed a large boulder and managed to get up slowly, taking in deep breaths. I was so close to Jesus that I could see His sweat mixed with blood pouring out from the pores of His skin. There was a pool of blood at the foot of the cross. Leaning against the rock, I sobbed while trying to keep my balance. I could feel the crowd's anger intensify as I began to throw up.

Trying to regain my composure, I looked up and noticed Jesus' eyes were closed, yet His lips were moving. Perhaps He was praying. I watched Him closely, wanting to hear every word. *Is He praying for the people? Is He praying for Himself? Is He praying for me?* Just then He lifted His head and gazed directly into my eyes. He looked deeply into my soul with such compassion, appearing more concerned about me than Himself. I started to cry, feeling overwhelmed by His love. Yet, many in the crowd couldn't see what I saw as they shook their fists while yelling out obscenities. They couldn't see Jesus' heart as He looked upon them with such sorrow and remorse. He bowed His head as His lips whispered from above the noise of the crowds, "Father, forgive them. They know not what they're doing." (Luke 23:34)

That's when I woke up. I was back in the hospital. Mom was sitting in a chair talking to Paige on her cell phone. I noticed Dad was also with me watching TV. My sheets felt cold and wet as sweat trickled down the back of my neck. Images of Jesus on the cross flashed through my mind as I closed my eyes, trying to hold back my tears.

There was knock on our door. It was Dr. Canon.

"Hello, Mr. and Mrs. Allen. Hello, Jordan." Dr. Canon came over to my bedside and pulled up a chair. "Hey, how are you feeling?" He gently removed the mask from my face and wiped my forehead.

"G,ga," I tried to speak but could barely make any sounds.

"You're such a brave, strong young man."

I looked deeply into his eyes, picturing his soul wandering aimlessly on the pathway to Hell. *How could a brilliant surgeon become so lost? How would God use me to steer him back to Heaven's pathway?*

"Dr. Canon," Mom said, "how long does Jordan have to use a breathing treatment?"

"Not much longer; at least until the end of the week. We don't want him to struggle with breathing. It's simply precautionary. Once his numbers have increased, we can start weaning him off."

I felt something in my side and tried to grab it.

"That's your feeding tube Jordan," Dr. Canon responded smiling. "Don't pull that out. You might get hungry later."

"What's all of this medication you're giving him?" Mom asked.

"Chemo and several antibiotics to help prevent infection. We also have him on a mild pain medication to keep him comfortable."

"How long before we can go home?" Sam asked.

Dr. Canon looked up. "I don't know the answer to that question. I still don't know what Jordan's prognosis will be. I'm sorry."

I didn't like the sound of that. Dr. Canon didn't know what was going to happen to me. Only God could answer that question. As I looked over at the monitors, I didn't feel human any more. Feeding tubes, breathing machines; a lot of equipment was attached to my body. I closed my eyes, hoping to escape from my physical state. I wanted to be healed. I needed to feel God's presence. I needed to hear Michael tell me it was going to be OK. I felt so far away from God's Place of Rest; becoming more afraid of the unknown. I tried to focus my thoughts on a tiny little mustard seed, reminding me how a little faith is all I needed to get me through each day.

Just as I finished that thought, a tingling, cold sensation ran down my spine. I wasn't sure if I was awake or asleep, but someone else had entered the room. I tried opening my eyes, but couldn't. Instinctively I knew it was a demon. Instantly, my spirit was yanked from my body and dragged down the hospital corridor. I tried to scream as my soul was carried off to a graveyard and thrown into a coffin. *Am I dreaming? Is this really happening?* When I opened my eyes, all I could see was the inside walls of a black box. Darkness surrounded me. Frantically, I pounded my fists on the casket, screaming for someone to rescue me.

"Jesus, don't let me die! Don't leave me here. Please save me!"

Boom! The lid of the coffin flew open as rays of white light poured in. A hand reached inside and pulled me out.

"You belong to me, Jordan. Nothing will ever snatch you from the palm of My hand, not even death."

When I opened my eyes, I wasn't in the hospital but had returned to God's Place of Rest. Still shaken, I slowly got up and looked around. The demons were gone. Boy, was I ever grateful for that. I noticed a huge vineyard in the distance that I hadn't seen before. It was like looking at a painting, with the beautiful Heavenly Mountain in the backdrop. The vineyard stretched for miles, and from where I was standing, I could see the branches covered in clusters of grapes. The sky was crystal blue as God's glory poured down from the mountain onto the vineyard.

"Thank you, God! Thank you for saving me!" I took in a deep breath and headed towards the vineyard, hoping to find Michael. As I got closer, I noticed the leaves on the plants were a vibrant green and not one was damaged or torn. The smell of roses surrounded me, but none were in sight. I felt an inner peace that I didn't have in the hospital. The difficult part was accepting the fact that God's outcome may be different from what I wanted. I could see myself miraculously healed and telling the world my story. Maybe even a movie would be made about my life and how others turned to Christ through my journey. Although my plan seemed logical, accepting God's plan for my life meant accepting His ways were beyond my ways. Since He was the Creator of the universe, I had to believe He knew what He was doing.

I sat down for a moment and prayed. "Heavenly Father, thank you for God's Place of Rest. Thank you for always having a purpose even when things don't go my way. Help me to trust you no matter what. In Jesus' name, amen."

Chapter Ten

Prayers are Powerful

Rosalyn's Story

Three months had passed since Jordan was admitted, and every day was a fight to keep him alive. I knew in my heart God could take Jordan at any time, but it had to be up to Him and not our doctors.

Day after day, I closely monitored the medical activity concerning Jordan. Several mistakes occurred causing a sense of distrust between me and the staff. One involved a sudden decrease in Jordan's blood sugar levels. Despite our protesting for insulin, our request was refused. Jordan went into cardiac arrest, but thankfully survived. Sadly it took a crisis before doctors agreed to treat him.

Most days, Jordan rested peacefully and occasionally opened his eyes. He seemed completely content under these difficult circumstances. I knew he was the kind of boy who would fight to the end.

"Good morning, Mrs. Allen." Dr. Canon walked in. "And how are you doing today, Jordan?"

Jordan struggled to open his eyes and raised his left thumb. This was his way of saying hello.

"Dr. Canon, when will Jordan be discharged? We're ready to go home."

"Now that his breathing has normalized, we need to do a swallowing test to see if he's able to eat on his own. I'll get that scheduled."

"What about the tumor?"

"I wouldn't recommend any more radiation to the brain, but we will continue chemo. He's handling it well." Dr. Canon said forcefully. "Mrs. Allen, your son has overcome many milestones. I know you've been here a long time, and I know you want to go home, but we have to be realistic in our assessment."

"And what is your assessment?"

"Mrs. Allen, this is a very serious and lethal kind of cancer he's fighting."

"We are fully aware of that."

Dr. Canon looked at Rosalyn with no expression. "Unless you have any more questions, I need to make my rounds."

"I do have one more question, Dr. Canon." I hesitated for a moment. "Do you believe in God?"

Dr. Canon looked long into Rosalyn's eyes. "I don't know what my beliefs have to do with Jordan's treatment."

"They have everything to do with his care. Don't you pray for God's guidance, or do you simply rely on your personal expertise?"

"Mrs. Allen, in all due respect, I've seen this tumor before."

Just then a sound came from the bed. Jordan was trying to talk.

"Hey, are you OK, son?" Dr. Canon asked.

Jordan tried to speak as he reached for Dr. Canon's hand.

Rosalyn came over to the other side of the bed. "Jordan, what are saying? What do you need? Use your words Jordan. I know you can." Jordan looked at his mom and tried to whisper one word.

"Sar."

Dr. Canon squeezed Jordan's hand and turned to leave the room.

"Sar," Jordan said again.

"Sar-a," Rosalyn repeated. "Sar, sar, Sarah? Are you saying Sarah?"

Dr. Canon stopped at the door and turned around. Jordan was staring at him.

"Sar, Sarah? Jordan, what are you saying?" his mom asked.

Dr. Canon walked back over to Jordan and leaned over.

"Sa, Sarah," Jordan said.

Rosalyn stepped back as Dr. Canon leaned closer. "Jordan, are you saying Sarah?"

Jordan squeezed his hand.

Dr. Canon stared with a blank expression.

"What is it?" Rosalyn asked. "Who's Sarah, Jordan? We don't know anyone named Sarah."

"I'll be back later," Dr. Canon said as he hastily left the room. As he headed down the corridor, his mind was racing. *Did Jordan say Sarah? No, that's not possible. Did I ever mention Sarah's name in front of him or his family? No, I am certain of that. Was this just a mere coincidence? Perhaps a nurse on the floor was named Sarah or another doctor.* He had to find out.

Racing to his office as images of Sarah flooded his mind, he shut the door and pulled up every note, every doctor and nurse who treated Jordan, yet not one had the name Sarah. *Maybe Jordan was dreaming or perhaps talking about one of his friends, yet Mrs. Allen said they didn't know anyone named Sarah. Was Jordan hallucinating?* Dr. Canon rubbed his temples, recalling Jordan's expression as he looked at him. He didn't seem to be hallucinating. He took a deep breath and shrugged it off. He still had rounds to do and headed down the hospital corridor.

It was then an angel appeared and placed his arm around Dr. Canon. Overwhelmed by emotions, Dr. Canon raced into a nearby restroom to regroup.

***

Jordan's Story

As I looked upon the endless rows of grapes, I was overwhelmed by the size of the vineyard and the few workers who were working in the fields.

"Jordan, there you are. A beautiful vineyard, isn't it?" Michael showed up holding two baskets. I was thrilled to see him.

"Why aren't there more workers?"

"That's a good question," Michael said, looking in every direction.

"It seems like the owner of the field could use some more help."

"There's no doubt about it."

"Maybe I could help. I'm only a kid, but I can pick grapes."

"What a wonderful idea! They certainly could use your help."

I grabbed Michael's basket and headed down a row.

"Wow, look at these grapes! I've never seen anything so beautiful and perfectly shaped. These grapes look a lot different than what you see in a store!" I laughed heartily.

"That's because they aren't ordinary grapes. They represent the fruit produced from God's Kingdom Children." Michael smiled as he handed me a cluster.

"What do you mean?"

"The grape is symbolic of the fruit produced by Kingdom Children. First, the seed of faith is planted. Then if it takes root, fruit is produced. God is the vine and His children are the branches. The vine feeds the branches. If the branches produce fruit, God prunes and nourishes them so that the fruit becomes abundant," Michael explained.

I studied the grapes while pondering Michael's words. "What happens to the branches that don't produce fruit?"

"They're cut off and thrown into the fire."

My face fell at the sound of Michael's words.

"Fruit can only be produced through the power of the Holy Spirit. If one doesn't receive Christ, one doesn't receive His Spirit. Without His Spirit, there's no fruit."

As I studied the faces of those on the pathway to Hell, I was amazed how completely oblivious they were to what was ahead of them. And sadly, the Heavenly Mountain was in plain sight. My heart hurt for them. "I know there isn't another way to Heaven. I just wish Hell wasn't an option."

"Hell was never meant for mankind," Michael replied. "It was originally designated for Satan and his fallen angels."

I looked out at the masses and noticed the one thing that divided the Kingdom Children from everyone else. It wasn't race, socio economic status, or education. It was one's set of beliefs. You either believed in Christ, or not. That was the ultimate dividing factor.

"Michael, I had a dream about Jesus' death. It was terrible! Was it just a dream or something more?"

Michael was quiet for a long time until finally he broke the silence. "Pray and ask for Him to answer your question."

I remembered many of the faces in the crowd, shouting and mocking Jesus. People of all races and religions were there; some believers, but most were not. As Jesus looked at the people, His eyes were filled with love and compassion. He'd taken on the sin of mankind and received the penalty of death for everyone, regardless of their race or beliefs, yet not everyone would receive Him for who He really was. And those people represented the ones wandering aimlessly on the pathway to destruction.

I closed my eyes and began to pray. "Dear Lord, help me to understand everything that's happening. And help me to be all that you need me to be." I said it again; the very prayer that started my journey. But this time when I prayed, I truly meant it. Suddenly, something inside felt different. I really wanted to help others find the right pathway. I wanted God to use me in powerful ways and make a difference in someone's life. I thought about what Jesus said, "Father, forgive them. They don't know what they're doing."

When I opened my eyes, I noticed a few workers walked by and smiled.

"They seem happy. They must like working in the vineyard."

"That's true. They love doing God's work."

"You mean God is their boss?"

"God is everyone's boss, although many refuse to see it that way."

I watched closely how Michael would delicately pluck each grape from its branch, placing it gently in the basket as though it were fragile to the touch.

"What are the grapes used for?"

"Communion. We make wine from the grapes to honor what Jesus did for us on the cross."

I took one of the grapes and held it up to the light. It was perfectly shaped without bruise or defect of any kind. Its skin was a deep vibrant purple, with a hint of red glimmering inside its veins. I noticed some of the juice from the grapes had poured out in my basket. It reminded me of the blood that poured out of Jesus' body. I closed my eyes, trying not to think about it. It was the most horrifying thing I'd ever seen.

"Michael, Jesus didn't have to be crucified, did he?"

"No. He chose to."

"But why did He have to die such a horrible and painful death?"

"Sin is a horrible and detestable act against God, and all sin leads to death. That's why Jesus came and placed upon Himself all the sins of the world. He was crushed for your iniquities and pierced for your transgressions. His death was the only sacrifice acceptable to God."

"And Jesus knew many wouldn't believe in Him even though He chose to give up His life for them."

"Jordan, you must remember God's deepest desire is not to lose one of His children. God so loved the world that He gave up His only Son so that those who believe would not perish but have eternal life."

"And my suffering might also save someone?"

"Everything that happens in life, both good and bad can be used to further God's kingdom on earth. There are no coincidences."

A part of me was scared to return to my physical state, but if this was part of God's plan for my life, then I had to trust Him and believe He's got my back. Michael told me God would always have the final say.

"I'm ready." I hugged Michael tightly. I knew he'd be with me, and that made me less afraid. As I closed my eyes, I felt my spirit leaving the vineyard.

"Don't worry, Jordan. You're never alone. Jesus is always with you and I also have been commanded to protect you." I was comforted by Michael's words as I left God's Place of Rest.

Chapter Eleven
_____

Returning Home

Rosalyn's Story

We finally received word Jordan was being
discharged. Another miracle had happened.
Christmas was around the corner and we
would be home to celebrate. God had
answered our prayer. I'd been in the hospital
so long, I'd forgotten what it was like to have
a home cooked meal and sleep in my own
bed.

*Heavenly Father, thank you for this
day. Thank you for every day. We couldn't
have done it without You. Thank you for
another Christmas with Jordan.*

***

Jordan's Story

When I returned, my body was
propped up in a wheel chair, surrounded by

pillows. We were waiting on final paperwork. I couldn't wait to go home and see my room! And I couldn't wait to eat *real* food. My body was still weak, but hopefully, in time, I would regain my strength. Mom was talking to a nurse when Dr. Canon stopped by.

"Hey, Jordan, today's the day!" Dr. Canon said smiling "How are you feeling, son?"

"G-good," I said. Speaking was still very difficult.

"You keep doing what you're doing, alright?"

Just then Michael appeared. He walked over to me unnoticed by anyone else and placed his finger on my lips.

"Tell Dr. Canon about Sarah," Michael said.

I didn't think Dr. Canon would understand me. I looked at Michael curiously as he read my thoughts.

"God will help you; just trust Him," Michael said.

"You OK, Jordan?" Dr. Canon asked.

"Sa-Sar-Sarah," I said. "I ma-me-met your da-daughter."

"What did you say? You met Sarah?" Dr. Canon leaned closer to me. My parents were occupied with the nurses gathering all of my medical supplies.

"Sa-Ser-Sah-Sarah is in Heaven. I saw her." Just then, Sarah was standing next to

Michael. She looked so beautiful.

"Jordan, you've been through a lot," Dr. Canon said. "Some of the medication you're taking can cause strange dreams, maybe even hallucinations."

"Hi, Jordan," Sarah said.

I looked at her and lifted my hand towards her, trying to wave.

"What are you looking at, Jordan?" Dr. Canon asked.

"Ser-sa-Sarah. She's here."

"Jordan, tell Dad my nickname. He used to call me Peanut," Sarah said, smiling.

"Pee-pa-nut, Pea-nut. You called Sarah Peanut."

Dr. Canon couldn't believe what he heard. *How would Jordan know such a thing?*

"Dr. Canon, I have all the paperwork. Can we leave now?" Mom interrupted our conversation.

I looked into Dr. Canon eyes, and with every ounce of strength, I reached for his hand. Tears formed in the corner of the doctor's eyes, which he wiped with his fingers before facing Mom.

"Yes. Mrs. Allen, you're all set. Sorry to run but I need to check on another patient right now." Dr. Canon leaned over and squeezed Jordan's hand. "You hang in there, Jordan. I want to see continued progress out of you."

I motioned Dr. Canon to come closer

so I could hug him. He held me for a long time. Maybe, just maybe, he believed me. When I looked up, Sarah and Michael were gone. Dr. Canon headed down the hallway as Mom collected our remaining items. Dad was getting the car and we were finally going home.

***

Dr. Canon slipped into his office, closed the door, and sat down in his chair, wiping the tears on his cheeks. He looked over at a picture of Sarah with her mother. He missed her so much. *Did Jordan really see her? Is Heaven for real? How would Jordan have known her nickname?*

He got up, trying to gain composure. Surely this was a coincidence. *Many parents call their children Peanut, and Sarah was a common ordinary name. Is there really a Heaven?* His mind was racing with questions. Dr. Canon grabbed his clipboard and headed out to see his next patient, wanting to forget what happened.

As he walked down the hallway, he stopped and noticed the chapel just past his office. For over fifteen years, he never once stepped inside. He stared at the stained glassed window displaying an image of Jesus. It was made up of tiny pieces of radiant colored glass, capturing the sunlight as it poured through each piece. He recognized the Scripture embedded at the base of Jesus' feet. It was John 3:16, a Bible verse he memorized as a small child. *"For God so loved the world, that he gave his one and only son, that whoever believes in him shall not perish but have eternal life."*

Dr. Canon quietly recited the Scripture several times in his head, focusing on each word. God didn't just love the world, but He "so" loved the world. That simple word, 'so', pierced his heart. After Sarah's death, Dr. Canon couldn't see how a God of love could allow a young child to die. Yet God so loved the world, He allowed His one and only Son to die.

That he gave his one and only son...but why? He asked himself. *That whoever believes in him shall not perish, but have eternal life.*

Dr. Canon pondered this statement before realizing he'd opened the door and walked inside.

The chapel was empty, which seemed strange, especially in the middle of the day. Yet, the quietness of the sanctuary was so inviting. The soft lights and candlelight created a peaceful atmosphere, strikingly different from the hospital. He glanced at his watch and noted he was an hour ahead of schedule. He laughed to himself, trying to recall the last time he had a free hour. He slowly approached the front pew and sat down. His last memory of church was Sarah's funeral, leaving him bitter and angry at God.

Dr. Canon breathed in several deep breaths, trying to calm his nerves. The fragrance of flowers filled the room. There were roses and carnations placed in vases at each end of the altar. The aroma was much more pleasing than the hospital smells he was accustomed to. He leaned his head back on the pew, closed his eyes and fell into a deep sleep.

He dreamt about sitting in a church, observing a man face down crying at Jesus' feet. Jesus gently placed his hand on the man's shoulder.

Why's he crying? Dr. Canon asked himself. He watched Jesus trying to calm his emotions, but the man's tears wouldn't stop flowing. Dr. Canon sensed the man was afraid to look directly into Jesus' eyes, yet there wasn't a single trace of judgment in Jesus' expression. In fact, what Dr. Canon saw was an outpouring of love and compassion towards this broken man.

The man knew there was nothing he could hide from His Savior. Jesus could see into his soul, as each moment of the man's life was played back like a movie. Dr. Canon noticed pictures of the man's life were cut out like puzzle pieces hanging on the walls. Then it dawned on him, this man was no stranger, he was looking at himself.

Dr. Canon got up from the pew and studied each picture closely before realizing it was his life displayed in the puzzle pieces. The images ranged from his childhood to adulthood. Jesus and the man sat down together on the floor and began putting the pieces together.

As Dr. Canon studied each piece, something appeared in each one he'd never seen before. Jesus was present in every piece. His presence shone like a radiant light around the events displayed. You could see the light of Christ in the birthday celebrations, baseball games, and school dances. Jesus was there for holidays, graduations, and dinner parties. Yet as his years past, the light of Christ had faded; the images became increasingly darker compared to his childhood pieces.

Dr. Canon felt a deep pain in his heart as Jesus handed him a particular puzzle piece revealing Sarah's death. It was the darkest piece of all, yet even in the midst of the darkness, you could see a tiny glimmer of light as it cast a shadow over Sarah. Dr. Canon held the piece, as his eyes filled with tears. He studied it closely, confused because it didn't fit with the other pieces. He tried to maneuver it by turning the piece every which way, but nothing worked. He even tried forcing two pieces together, but with no success. Frustration grew as he desperately tried to fit this puzzle piece with the others. Finally, he gave up, exasperated by his efforts. Dr. Canon looked into Jesus' eyes hoping He would show him how this piece would connect with the others. Perhaps the meaning behind Sarah's death would finally be revealed, but that didn't happen.

"Show me how it fits!" Dr. Canon cried out. "I tried to fit it with the other pieces, but it doesn't work!"

Just when all hope seemed lost, Jesus spoke. "That's because the puzzle piece that joins them is missing."

Startled, Dr. Canon woke up from his dream, whipping his head around to see if anyone had entered the chapel, but no one had. Everything appeared normal. He sat quietly in the pew and glanced at his watch. Only thirty minutes had passed, yet it felt like he was asleep for hours.

What piece was missing? Dr. Canon wondered while looking at a painting of Jesus on the chapel wall, reading it once more. *"And God so loved the world that He gave His only Son that whoever believes in Him shall not perish, but have eternal life."*

Ahhh, it came to him. *The pieces from my childhood fit together because my faith was interwoven into each event. But as I grew older, I chose the busyness of life over spending time with God. And the more I distanced myself from God, the darker the pieces became. When Sarah died, my faith died with her, leaving a missing piece. Faith in Christ was needed to connect both the joys and sorrows.* Looking closely at the puzzle piece, he noticed a tiny dim light shining in the background. Goosebumps cover his body as it dawned on him, *Although I abandoned my faith, Jesus had never abandoned me.*

Broken in remorse and regret, he bowed his head in prayer, something he hadn't done in a long time. He was so humbled by God's love and devotion despite his anger and resentment towards Him. He'd wanted nothing to do with God after Sarah's death. Then he recalled Jesus's expression as he cried at His feet. Jesus would forgive him and take him back, as one of His own, without hesitation. Christ had never turned His back on him. As Dr. Canon sat quietly, he remembered that just before Sarah died, she had a special prayer she shared with him. He was so moved by her words, asking Jesus to take care of her parents. Sarah was more concerned about their wellbeing than she was about dying.

"I'm so sorry, Jesus. I'm so sorry," he whispered quietly. Although he didn't understand Sarah's death, he knew this puzzle piece would someday reveal a grandeur plan for his life.

Walking out into the hospital corridor, his heavy heart was gone. As he glanced back at the stained glass door, Dr. Canon promised to return to the chapel daily as part of his hospital rounds. He raced towards the entrance of the hospital, hoping to find Jordan.

Rosalyn and Sam were loading up the car when they heard Jordan's name.

"Jordan!" Dr. Canon called out.

"Dr. Canon, is everything ok?" Sam asked. Rosalyn opened up the car door and got out.

Dr. Canon stuck his head inside the window and smiled at Jordan.

"Thank you, Jordan." Tears were brimming in Dr. Canon's eyes; a different person now resided there. His soul seemed to be at peace.

I smiled as I silently thanked God for what He did. I wasn't the only one returning home. Dr. Canon would find his way also.

Dad opened the car door and I hugged Dr. Canon. Tears were streaming down both our cheeks. My cancer truly had made a difference in someone's life.

***

Rosalyn's Story

As we drove into our neighborhood, we passed Jordan's school where hundreds of kids and teachers waved banners and cheered as we passed by. We pulled up into the driveway and were welcomed by several relatives waiting for our arrival.

We came home to a drastically different life. A hospital bed was placed in Sam's and my bedroom downstairs to monitor Jordan twenty-four hours a day. Oxygen tanks and prescription bottles filled our rooms. Our home looked like a hospital as nurses came by each day, and so we faced new challenges, learning simple daily tasks that were no longer simple for Jordan. He was completely dependent on us for eating, bathing, and mobility. Despite these setbacks, we were thrilled to be home for Christmas. God had answered our prayers.

Chapter Twelve

The Armor of God

Rosalyn's Story

Jordan rested peacefully while many nights I sat by his bedside, monitoring his breathing and praying for a miracle. Jordan was so brave. Therefore, I needed to be brave also. We no longer had the luxury of a medical team that would come at the push of a button. It was primarily me and Sam. Bear, and Paige were also a big help in creating a new routine for our family. It took two of us to get him out of bed and ready for breakfast. Each morning, Jordan would wake up early, adamant we not waste time lying in bed. Most teenagers loved to sleep away their days, but not Jordan. He would call out and insist we get up, even at 5:00 am. Jordan could never be alone, so that meant we all took shifts to help him with walking, sitting, eating, and encouraging him to stay positive. We didn't know his prognosis, so we had to live each day in the moment.

One morning while cooking breakfast, I noticed a stack of mail on the kitchen counter. I hadn't opened the mail in weeks. Thumbing through it, I found a certified letter from one of Jordan's doctors. I assumed it was bad news. *Why would a doctor send a certified letter?* As I read its contents, I felt like a knife stabbed my heart. Jordan's doctor informed us she would no longer provide care for our son. I stared at the letter in disbelief. *How could anyone choose to simply walk away from this! We have come so far!* There was another letter from the insurance company. I opened it slowly, anticipating the worst. The letter stated our family had become an expense and they were threatening to discontinue coverage. Paralyzed by fear, I stood motionless in the kitchen, sobbing. "Dear Lord. What are we going to do? What are we going to do?"

***

Jordan's Story

I woke up to the sound of Mom crying in the other room. I pretended to be asleep as Dad got out of bed and went out to the kitchen to comfort her. I overheard my parents talking about my situation. Taking care of me was like taking care of a two-month-old baby, except I was over one hundred pounds. I could no longer walk, bathe, or feed myself without their help, and wondered if I had become a burden both physically and now financially.

"Jordan, you're awake." Mom walked in the room, pretending nothing was wrong. "How's my beautiful boy?" She kissed me on the forehead while she and Dad placed me in my wheel chair and rolled me to the living room. My sister Paige was watching TV. She ran over and kissed my hand. She always had a smile on her face.

"Paige, you doin' OK?" I asked.

Paige looked at me and smiled. "Yeah, I'm good."

We sat quietly for a moment watching TV before I spoke again. "Are you scared?"

"Scared of what?"

"That I might die?"

"You won't die, silly." Paige hugged me. It used to irritate her when I hugged her, but now she was hugging me all the time. Paige was more than my little sister, she was my best friend.

"Paige," I said quietly.

"What?"

"I'm glad God allowed this to happen to me and not you. I don't know if you could handle it."

Paige held my hand without saying anything. I decided I would never talk about my condition again with her. I wanted our time together to be as normal as possible. Besides, she was right. Death doesn't exist for the Christian believer.

We ate breakfast and headed to physical therapy. Afterwards, we went out to eat at a restaurant of my choice. Burgers and fries always hit the spot. We would try to be normal and not talk about cancer. Mostly we laughed a lot. Once Mom tried to steal my french-fries. I reminded her that even though I couldn't speak well, I could still see with no problem. She looked at me and we laughed until we cried.

When we got home, I was exhausted. Mom helped me go to the restroom before lying down for a nap. While washing my hands, I looked at myself in the mirror and was shocked to see how different I looked. I could barely smile because even my face was partially paralyzed. I took in a deep breath, trying not to focus on my condition.

Mom propped me up in bed as I closed my eyes, hoping to return to God's Place of Rest, praying, *Thank you God for being with me and my family. Please don't allow me to be too much of a burden. Please take care of my family. Help me to be strong.*

As I fell asleep, a warm sensation came over me. Something deep inside told me Jesus was in the room. I could feel His love as tears of gratitude trickled down my face. His hand softly touched my cheeks and wiped my tears away. *Please don't ever leave me, Jesus.*

I'm always with you Jordan. I'll never leave you. Don't let your heart be troubled.

His voice spoke deep inside my heart, filling me with confidence that everything would be just fine.

I slowly opened my eyes and was surprised to see Jesus was on my bedside, smiling. He was the most beautiful being I'd ever seen, even more beautiful than Michael. He wore a long, light-blue gown and His eyes glistened like emeralds. I studied Him for a long time before I could speak.

"Jesus, I'm scared about everything that's happening. I'm scared of the evil one. I want to be brave like Michael or even Sarah, but I'm not," I confessed.

"Would you believe me if I told you Satan was more afraid of you?"

"How can that be?"

"Come, I want to show you something."

Immediately, my spirit left my parent's bedroom. I was standing knee deep in a river beside Jesus. The water was crystal blue and it felt refreshingly cool on my legs. It was so clear I could see my toes standing on the rocks. Jesus was smiling.

"Wow! It's really amazing! The water is like nothing I've ever seen before. But why are we standing in it?"

"Would you like to be baptized, Jordan?" Jesus replied.

Dumbstruck, it dawned on me I'd never been baptized.

"Yes! That would be cool."

"Well, this would be the perfect time to do it. Are you ready?"

"Yes," I said excitedly. I was going to be baptized by Jesus Christ Himself! I couldn't wait to tell my parents about this!

Jesus lifted me in his arms and gently knelt down while completely submerging me into the water. When I opened my eyes under the water, rays of different colored light surrounded me as though I was inside a rainbow. He lifted me out of the water while looking up into the sky, praying to God. He gently placed me back on my feet in the water. I hugged him closely, never wanting this moment to end. However, when I glanced across the water, I was terrified by what I saw.

"Jesus! The Devil is behind you with an army of demons!" Satan was glaring at us. I clung tightly to Jesus.

"He's here only because I allow it," Jesus replied, looking over at the evil one.

"But why? Why do you allow it?"

"Satan is allowed to rule for a period of time, but his power is restricted."

"Why is he so frightening?"

"Because you allow him to be frightening. Fear is a tool he uses to intimidate you."

"Well, it works."

"The power in you is far greater than the power in him. You are a Kingdom Child. Your life is in the palm of My hands."

"Why does he keep showing up then?"

"Because he wants to destroy every human being, but those baptized by both water and Spirit pose the greatest threat to him. When the devil sees you, he also sees Me in you. That's why you're a threat to him. I have been given all authority over Heaven and Earth."

"What happened to him? Why is he so angry at God's children?"

"You have something he will never have again."

"What's that?"

"Eternal life in Heaven. Satan used to be the most powerful and majestic angel in the Heavenly kingdom, but pride overtook him. The Father will not share His glory with anyone," Jesus replied.

"So God removed him from Heaven?"

"Yes. He was thrown out of Heaven along with his followers and has been roaming on the earth for thousands of years...but his time will soon come to an end."

"He's so big and powerful. I'm just a young kid."

"No, Jordan, you are more than a young kid. You're a Kingdom Child. Turn around and tell me what you see."

Satan was watching us closely as I did what He said. There were hundreds, maybe thousands of God's mighty angels standing along the shoreline and Michael was in the center with his sword in hand.

"Whoa! Now that's an army of angels!"

"Yes, it is, and they are commanded to protect God's Kingdom Children," Jesus responded. "That's what the armor of God looks like and it is available to every believer."

"What are they waiting on? Aren't they going to attack Satan's army?"

Jesus smiled as He turned to look where Satan was standing. To my amazement, Satan and his demons had vanished. Not one remained.

"They're gone!" I replied excitedly. "Where did they go?"

"They fled."

"I'm glad I'm on your side, Jesus."

"Me, too, Jordan."

As I placed my arms around My Father, I tried to wrap my head around the fact He was man as much as He was God. I held His hands, touching the scars where the nails were driven in. I thought about my dream, seeing Him hanging on the cross as the people screamed and mocked Him. My heart was filled with every kind of emotion. I was sad that He died such a horrible death, but grateful that He died for me. I was sad for so many who mocked Him and didn't know who Jesus was, and overjoyed for those who believed and repented. Grateful to know my salvation was secured, but sad for those who were on the pathway to Hell. So many had no idea who Jesus was and what His life and death meant to mankind. I grieved for their souls knowing many may never know the truth.

"I'm sorry. I'm sorry for my sin and all the bad things I did. I'm sorry for all You went through."

"It was worth it." He smiled so lovingly. The light surrounding Him became so intensely bright I had to close my eyes. When I opened them, I was back at home in my bed. Jesus was sitting on my bedside. I gazed at Him in amazement, never wanting this moment to end.

"Don't be afraid, Jordan. Don't let your heart be troubled." Those were His last words before leaving my room.

"Hey, Jordan, you're awake. Are you hungry?" Mom was sitting next to me, smiling. She looked so peaceful. If only she knew Jesus had been sitting just on the opposite side of her.

"Ma-mom, I wan to be bapti—," I struggled so hard with my words.

"What's wrong? Speak slowly."

"Baptis—baptized. I wan to be baptized this Sunday!" I said, relieved I finally got the words out.

"Seriously? But why? Why now?"

"Jesus wants me to. Let's do it this Sunday."

"I'll call and see what we can do."

"Promise, Mom?"

"Yes, sweetie, I promise," Rosalyn responded.

As I watched her leave the room, I thought about my baptism with Jesus. Coming out of the water changed me from the inside out. Physically my body was growing weaker, but spiritually I was forever changed. Too much significance is placed on the physical life when what we should be concerned about is our spiritual life. I was made new in Christ and no disease could ever take that away from me.

***

Rosalyn's Story

God did it. The church rearranged Sunday's services to include the baptism of both Jordan and Paige. Nothing was more special than seeing my children baptized together. We watched Jordan and Paige on a huge television screen being dunked into a large pool of water inside the church. Several young men held him closely. When Jordan came out of the water, you could see the joy beaming from his face. Paige hugged her brother and wiped his face, a moment I would always cherish.

After the service, family and friends came by the house to celebrate the day's events. After everyone left, Sam and I helped Jordan get ready for bed. For the first time in many weeks, I felt an inner peace despite my circumstances. How many fourteen-year-old teenagers demanded to be baptized? Something happened with Jordan. He said he spoke with Jesus and I believed him. More importantly, Jordan obeyed. Perhaps he and Jesus shared many conversations while in a coma.

As I looked at my son sleeping, I thought about the prayer I taught him: "Lord, help me be all that you need me to be." I knew in my heart Jordan wanted to play football. He had the dreams of any young teenage boy, but God's plan may be different. Maybe he would be healed, but there was a strong possibility he wouldn't. Sam and I sat in the other room and recapped our day. We both hoped this baptism would point to a new beginning.

While watching TV, suddenly I heard a gasping sound from our bedroom. Sam and I ran in to find Jordan wasn't breathing.

"Oh my God! Call 911!" I screamed.

Within minutes, two fireman were pounding on the front door. Paige let them in as they raced into the bedroom One leaned over Jordan and cried out, "He's not breathing! Get him on the floor!"

One fireman began pounding Jordan's chest, struggling to bring him back to life. I hugged Paige as we watched in complete shock.

"Please God, save Jordan! Please don't let him die!" Paige cried out to God.

"We got a heartbeat!" One of the firemen called out. "Get him on the stretcher. Let's go!"

We raced to the hospital. No one spoke a word in the car. Sam flew down the highway while Paige and I remained silent, paralyzed with fear.

***

Jordan's Story

Being baptized with Paige was amazing. Two teenagers helped me because I couldn't use my legs anymore. They sat with me in the water while the pastor prayed over me and Paige. As I looked out into the congregation, I wondered how many could see beyond my physical condition and look at me with spiritual eyes. Regardless of what the cancer had done on the outside, I had been born again on the inside. While under water, I pretended the cancer was washed away. It was like being in God's Place of Rest while here on earth. When I came up for air, I looked over at Paige whose face was lit up with joy. We hugged while she helped me out of the water. I felt so strong and wondered if I looked different to her? Could she see my healed spirit smiling? I looked for Michael in the crowd, but I couldn't see him, even though something told me he was there watching the event.

When we got home, my family gathered to celebrate. Some of my friends came by to say hello. While they talked among themselves, I wondered if any of them had actually been changed by their faith. *Would I see their souls along the pathway to Heaven or Hell? Did their parents even attend church or give God a second thought? If I could tell them everything I'd seen, would they think I was a nut case?* I closed my eyes and prayed for each of them, hoping not one of their souls would be left behind.

After a few hours, I was exhausted and went to lie down. Mom lifted me from the chair and placed me in bed. I weighed nearly ninety pounds and was amazed by her physical strength. She never once dropped me, although there were times I thought she might. She never complained about being tired, but I know it wasn't easy.

As I rested in bed, I could hear the voices in the other room laughing and talking about the day's events. I hadn't heard laughter in our house for quite some time. It was so good to know my family could still laugh despite everything that's happened. Soon after, everyone left and the house was quiet. Mom came in and kissed me on the forehead.

"I love you, sweetheart. I'm so proud of you."

I tried to smile as I closed my eyes, feeling groggy and weak. As much as I enjoyed today, I wanted to fall asleep and return to God's Place of Rest. I said a prayer to myself, *Heavenly Father, thank you for today. Please take care of my family. If I die, please don't let them be sad all the time. And please help them with any bills from my illness. Also, I pray Michael can be Paige's guardian angel. He's the best. Thank you Jesus.*

As the last word left my thought, a jabbing pain pierced my chest. I thought my heart would burst. I couldn't breathe as I tried to call out for help. I blacked out as memories of my childhood flooded my mind. I watched birthdays, holidays, and football games play out in my brain. Yet, in the background, I could hear Paige's voice.

"Jesus, please save Jordan. Please don't let him die."

What was happening? Was I dying?

A warm sensation came over me. My heart was beating again as I was lifted onto a stretcher and placed in an ambulance. When I opened my eyes, Michael was with me.

Where are we Michael? What's going on? I hoped Michael could read my thoughts.

"Come, Jordan. I want you to meet someone."

Instantly my spirit was carried away to God's Place of Rest.

***

Rosalyn's Story

Jordan had a heart attack. We took him to a different hospital because his former one refused care. He was stabilized, but in a coma again. It felt like we were back at square one, fearing for the worst.

Meanwhile, our new doctors spoke with Jordan's previous hospital team and familiarized themselves with our story. They appeared distant and guarded in their communication with us. I knew it would be a matter of time before they, too, would decide to discontinue any further treatment.

Two days had passed since Jordan was admitted. Nurses came in and out of the room, but no one was talking to us about their treatment plans. Finally, one of the doctors came by to share his assessment. Sam had left for work and Paige was in school. I was alone with Jordan.

"Good morning, Mrs. Allen. My name is Dr. Mann. How are we doing today?"

I looked up and smiled. "Fine, I suppose."

"Mrs. Allen, I'm leaving town tomorrow but will be back in ten days. By then, there is a strong probability your son will have passed away. Have you given any thought about donating his brain for further research?"

For a moment, I thought I was hallucinating. "What did you just ask me?"

"If we do further studies on his brain, we might learn what caused this," Dr. Mann said nonchalantly.

I slowly got out of my chair, shocked by his tone and disregard for my son's life.

"Get out of here, doctor! If Jordan dies, I will *never* give you his brain!"

Dr. Mann looked intently at me and walked out. I was boiling with anger, enraged by his words. He talked about Jordan's brain like it was some kind of commodity. A biopsy on his brain was more important than trying to save our son. I couldn't stop crying. *How did we get to this point?* "God, please help me! I can't do this anymore! Please, God, please! I need You to have the final say."

Once I was able to calm down, I called Sam and told him what happened. He raced to the hospital from work. In one moment, we were celebrating our children's baptism, and in the next moment, a doctor was asking me for my son's brain. Yesterday, I was on a mountaintop, but today we were once again in a valley facing the shadow of death. Sam and I opened our Bible and read Psalm 23. I tried desperately not to be afraid, reminding myself nothing was impossible for God.

Chapter Thirteen

The Vineyard Owner

Jordan's Story

I didn't know how long I was unconscious, but when I opened my eyes, my spirit was standing on the Heavenly Mountain with Michael. From up here, you could see all God's Place of Rest. The view was amazing. Fields of flowers covered the base of the mountain in every color of a rainbow and I could see the ocean and white sandy beaches in the far distance. On my right side was a vineyard like a purple sea of grapes. Animals grazed in the grassy fields. I wondered if this was what the world looked like from God's point of view.

"Amazing, isn't it?" Michael said as we stood silently, taking it all in. Looking up, I saw a beautiful rainbow. We were so high up, I thought I could touch it. Its brilliant colors poured over the people as they wandered along the pathways, yet many couldn't see it.

"They're so blind, and yet God's presence is all around them. How much time do they have?" I asked in disbelief.

"How much time do they need?" Michael responded. "Many live to be one hundred years old and never acknowledge God in their lives; others acknowledge Him at the age of five. God has made His presence known for thousands of years. No one will ever have the excuse for not knowing God."

"It breaks my heart to see so many on the wrong pathway," I said, holding back my tears.

"With wisdom comes sorrow. You now see things from a spiritual perspective. But remember, when there's breath, there's hope."

In the distance I saw a cloud shaped like a dove. Its wings hovered over the people like a blanket of protection. "What is that?"

"That's the Holy Spirit, Jordan."

"Why does He hover over those who are headed towards Hell? Some of the standstills haven't taken one step! They're exactly where they were when I first came here."

"God is in constant pursuit of his children. We might give up on God, but He never gives up on us. Remember what you've learned. Heaven rejoices when just one soul is saved."

"I wish I could have saved more."

"Your testimony of faith will have a rippling effect for years to come. You're only called to plant the seed."

I remembered I still had the bag of seeds in my pocket. I pulled it out and noticed there were a few seeds left. *Funny how such a tiny little seed became so significant in my life.* I thought about Dr. Canon and how his faith was restored. Sarah depended on me to help her dad and that required me to trust God with the details. Although I couldn't speak, somehow God would speak through me. There was nothing more awesome than being used by God to further His kingdom.

"Jordan, let's go to the vineyard. There's someone I want you to meet." Michael took my hand as we walked down the mountain. With a blink of an eye, the mountain was behind us.

"Angels sure have a way of getting around quickly," I said, giggling.

As we walked along, I noticed an elderly man in a wheel chair, praising God while struggling to maneuver himself up a hill. His arms and legs were thin as he slowly turned the wheels, and rocks kept getting caught inside. He struggled to go a few inches as he took in deep breaths along the way. Physically he seemed weak, and spiritually he was strong and determined. Nothing seemed to break this man's spirit as he slowly crawled along the pathway.

"He's not getting very far."

"No, he isn't. There are a lot of rocks in his way. His name is Leonard."

"How did he become crippled?"

"He was born that way."

I watched closely while Leonard struggled along. "Does he ever ask the Lord why he was born this way?"

"In the beginning he did."

"And what did God tell him?"

"The same thing He told you; to further His kingdom. God's strength would be revealed in his weakness."

"He seems happy, despite his situation." I smiled while watching Leonard. We shared something in common. Our suffering would be used to further God's kingdom. "God can use anyone, can't He?"

"Yes, that's true. But not everyone wants to be used by God."

Strangely, hundreds of people walked right past him, never offering assistance. Leonard was invisible to them. And others who saw Leonard purposely chose a different path to avoid helping him. However, Leonard continued praising God while inching along the pathway. I couldn't stand it any longer before marching over and offering assistance.

"Hi, my name is Jordan. May I push you over to where the pathway is less rocky?"

"Yes, thank you, son," the man said smiling. "I'm so grateful for your assistance."

I pushed Leonard along as Michael walked behind me.

"My name is Leonard."

"Yes, I know. My guardian angel told me."

Leonard looked at me strangely. "Are you also an angel?"

"No," I laughed, "I'm just a kid."

"Well, you seem like an angel to me." Leonard laughed and shook my hand. "Thanks again."

Right before our eyes, the rocks disappeared as the pathway became as smooth as glass. I looked at Michael to see if he noticed.

"What just happened? Did you see that, Leonard?"

"Yes, I did. God is good. Thank you, Jordan. I can make it the rest of the way," Leonard said smiling gratefully.

I watched him as he wheeled himself along. Then out-of-the-blue, Leonard stood on his own two feet. My mouth dropped open as he changed right before my eyes! Leonard wasn't a crippled man, but a beautiful angel surrounded by the light of God's glory.

"Michael, did you see that? He's an angel!" I looked around to see if others had noticed. "No one else saw him!" I cried out in disbelief.

"One person saw him," Michael responded smiling.

Just then I heard a voice behind me. "Hello, Jordan. I'm Christopher. I own the vineyard. I see you met Leonard."

"I didn't know he was an angel!'"

"And yet you responded the way Christ calls all of us to respond to the poor, the needy, and the sick. You took the time and helped someone, while others passed by. People come into our lives for a reason. and some may actually be angels. I could also use some extra help. Are you available?"

"Absolutely! Happy to." When I turned to look for Leonard and Michael, they were gone.

"Where did they go?"

"Angels work nonstop in protecting God's children. Come, let's go!" Christopher said jovially.

As I looked into Christopher's eyes, I noticed they sparkled like Michael's. There was something familiar about him, but I didn't know if we'd met. He was tall, slightly bronzed, and appeared to be in his thirties.

He handed me a basket as we walked toward a row of grapes. I watched closely as he diligently pruned each plant, even ones that looked dead. I remembered what Michael once told me: Jesus was the vine and the branches represented the children of God.

"Why are you pruning the dying ones? Shouldn't we focus on the healthy ones first?"

"Each branch is invaluable to me, even the ones that are dying. They don't have much time. Look at the unbelievers. Many are a breath away."

I turned and saw those standing just outside the eternal gates of Hell. I shuddered at the thought of spending one day in the lake of fire, separated from God forever.

"Do they ever get a second chance?"

"God gives multiple chances on earth. But when someone dies without receiving Christ as their Lord and Savior, their destination is final."

As I glanced down the row of plants, there were more dying ones than healthy ones. "What about the standstills, did they ever have faith?"

"That's a good question. They had faith, but it was dead faith."

Christopher words struck me deeply. "How's that?" I asked.

"Do you see that mulberry tree in the distance?"

I turned to look at a huge, beautiful tree that stood over fifty feet tall. "Yes, I see it."

"That particular tree is over one hundred years old. Its root system is nearly five hundred feet below the ground. Yet, according to the Bible, "If you have faith as small as a mustard seed, you can say to that mulberry tree, 'Be uprooted and planted in the sea,' and it will obey you. (Luke 17:6). Do you believe that, Jordan? Do you believe the power in you is capable of overcoming any problem, no matter how big it may seem?"

"All I know is nothing is impossible for God."

Christopher smiled and hugged me. "And that's all the faith you need. The standstills never believed what they said they believed. Many attended church, took Bible studies, and even went to seminary school, but Christianity was nothing more than a Sunday morning event."

"What do they have to do to get more faith?"

"It's not more faith they need, but a deeper faith from within. They need to believe in what God says!"

"If only they could see what I've seen, maybe that would change them."

"They've seen what you've seen. Miracles happen every day, but standstills refer to them as coincidences or even luck."

I thought about my parents and how strong their faith remained throughout my cancer. "Christopher, Mom still believes God could heal me if He wanted to."

"What do you believe?" He looked at me intently.

"I believe He could heal me, but it may not be His plan."

"And how do you feel about that? How do you feel about not playing professional football?"

I looked curiously at Christopher wondering how he would have known that about me. That dream seemed so long ago. So much had happened since then.

"You know Jordan, there was a time when even Jesus asked His Father to change His mind."

"Really? When was that?"

"Just before the soldiers came to arrest Jesus, He asked His Father if there could be another way. He was referring to his death. But then Jesus said, 'Not My Will, but Your Will be done'. Jesus knew God's plan is always better than our own."

"So Jesus knew He was going to die a horrible death, and He went through with it anyway," I said humbly.

"Yes, He did. A short time of pain and suffering would allow for many lives to be saved for eternity. Jesus knew the big picture behind God's plan. You may not fully understand His big picture for your suffering, but you must trust God knows what He's doing. The life of a Kingdom Child is not his own, but belongs to the Father for His purpose."

"If there's one thing I've learned, God's ways are not always our ways. But ultimately, I do believe His ways are better," I said smiling. "It's a privilege to be used by God, especially in my suffering. I got to help Dr. Canon, which was really cool, although a lot of people think my parents have gone off the deep end for keeping me alive."

"God is keeping you alive. He always has the final say. And believe it or not, Jesus' own family at one time thought He was crazy. Christians are called to be radically different from the world. Your parents are in good company!"

As I began picking the grapes, I thought back on my life before cancer. I used to care more about what my friends thought of me than what God thought of me. But none of that mattered now. "If I survive this, I hope I don't go back to my old ways. I will speak up for Christ, no matter what!"

"I believe you will, Jordan. I believe you will. How about something to eat? You must be getting hungry."

A basket of freshly baked bread, chocolates, and assorted fruit and cheeses appeared at my feet. One never goes hungry in God's Place of Rest. Christopher and I sat down to enjoy a meal. He broke the bread and gave thanks before handing me some. As I took it from his hand, I noticed what appeared to be a small scar resembling a nail hole. I looked into Christopher's eyes the same time I heard Michael's voice behind me.

"Michael, please join us. We're enjoying a snack," Christopher said.

"Thank you." Michael sat next to us.

While we ate, I watched the people wandering aimlessly along the pathways. I wondered if my condition would plant the seed of faith in any of them. I closed my eyes and said a prayer silently to myself. *God, please let me see one more soul saved from Hell.*

Chapter Fourteen

A Father's Love

Sam's Story

Rosalyn shared with me what Dr. Mann said. Paige and I remained in the waiting room because the hospital had limited the number of people allowed in Jordan's room. My mind was racing as I sat quietly staring at a TV screen. I could only shake my head in disbelief how anyone could ask to take Jordan's brain in the manner that he did. The thought was nauseating to me. He seemed to care more about studying Jordan's brain than treating it. At least Paige wasn't there to hear this conversation; she'd been traumatized enough seeing her brother suffer a heart attack. We certainly didn't want to add fuel to the fire. His condition was now stable but critical. We agreed Rosalyn would stay with him tonight. After several hours in the waiting room, I finally convinced Paige to come home with me and get a good night's sleep. Although she wanted to be with Jordan, I knew it would better for her to leave.

Our car ride home was silent as we drove down the highway in the middle of the night. Neither of us wanted to talk about Jordan's turn of events. I didn't have any words of comfort, so music became the buffer that calmed our emotional state. When we arrived home, Bear was waiting at the door. His name may have described his size, but his heart was soft and compassionate. Bear was always there when you needed him; the protector over Paige and Jordan. He attended all of Jordan's sporting events and spent endless hours playing hide and seek with the kids when they were young. Bear embraced Jordan's pain like it was his own.

Feeling shell shocked, we got out of the car and hugged for quite some time.

Paige didn't want to sleep alone, so she moved into our bedroom. We prayed together before I tucked her in. She fell right to sleep. I was grateful for that.

Bear was upstairs while I rested quietly on the bed, trying to make sense of everything. Yesterday started out as a celebration of Baptism and ended in a near death experience. Jordan was in a coma again, being treated by doctors who didn't know how to heal him. *How much more could Jordan endure? How much more could we endure?* Someone once told me God never gives us more than we can handle, but I've learned that's a lie. This was far more than my family could handle. Perhaps God purposely gives us more than we are capable of handling so that we turn to Him for strength instead of relying on ourselves.

God, when I grow up, I want to have faith like Jordan's, I said to myself. As a grown man, I now understood why God commands us to have childlike faith. I could see it in my own son. Jordan never questioned what was written in the Bible. Only those who didn't believe question what was written in the Bible. I couldn't make sense out of why God allowed Jordan to have cancer instead of me. He was the saint in our family, and yet his life was on the line. I may have been the head of the household, but Jordan was the pillar of faith.

Although I was proud of his accomplishments, it was his faith I admired most.

It should have been me! Why didn't you choose me! I prayed silently to myself. God knows I would have traded places with Jordan in a heartbeat.

The alarm clock went off. I couldn't recall if I'd slept as I watched the morning light come through the window blinds. It was after 3:00 am when we got home and now 7:00am appeared on my alarm clock. I looked over and saw Paige was still out like a light. I got out of bed, trying not to disturb her. My body ached as I walked to the kitchen to make coffee. This ordeal was draining, both physically and emotionally. Although it had been a year since Jordan became ill, it seemed like yesterday.

I stared out the kitchen window, drinking my coffee, amazed by the tranquility in my own backyard. The sky was painted with the colors of sunrise, while birds sang in the trees. I stepped onto the patio, feeling a chill in the air as it brushed against my cheeks. The outside world was completely unscathed by my family's year of turmoil. I sat down, thinking this was probably a good time to pray, but I couldn't. I was so exhausted, I couldn't think. My mind was foggy and my heart was numb as I tried to make sense of everything. I stared up into the sky and watched the sun's rays peek through the trees, slowly burning off the morning fog. The mist from the fog sparkled liked diamonds as the light touched it. A part of me didn't want to leave my patio. It was hard to see my son in his current condition. At times, he didn't look real to me, with all the tubes connected to his body. But I knew I had to return to the hospital and face our reality.

I finished my coffee and decided to stop by my office on the way. I needed to update my boss on Jordan's condition. He had been very supportive over all the days I'd missed work and I hoped he would remain that way.

As I drove down the highway, I listened to Christian music, trying to calm my nerves. The lyrics described trials as a way of becoming closer to God. My faith told me there was a divine plan behind this. *But even if I could understand it, is my faith strong enough to accept it? Faith tells me God can make good out of everything, but am I be able to see God's goodness in the death of my son? Faith tells me to rejoice in both joys and sorrows, but will I be able to rejoice without Jordan in my life?* The Bible told me I needed to have faith the size of a mustard seed, but right now my faith seemed smaller than a speck of dust resting on top of a mustard seed. The only thing I knew for sure was this journey would either reveal the depth of my faith or expose the lack of it.

I finally made it to the office and met with my boss. He told me to take care of Jordan over everything else. I was relieved, knowing my job wasn't in jeopardy, especially since I knew more days would be spent at Jordan's bedside.

After our visit, I headed towards the parking garage, trying to brace myself for what awaited at the hospital. My hands were shaking as I fumbled for my keys before opening the door of my truck. As I sat alone in a dark parking garage, I stared blankly out the window, taking in deep breaths. Memories of Jordan flooded my mind beginning with birthdays, vacations, and family reunions. *How can I live without my boy?! We did everything together! Why was this happening to me?!* I broke down and cried, consumed by my fear over Jordan possibly dying.

"Oh God, I beg you. Please save Jordan! Don't let him die! Please, God!" I cried out loud. "Are you punishing me, God? What if this was caused by my sin?" My mind went in every direction as I tried to make sense of this. *What have I done to deserve this! Take my life and spare Jordan's. I beg you God, please don't let him die!* My heart wept until I couldn't breathe. It felt like the wind had been knocked out of me.

"God, are you listening! Can you hear me!" I was screaming at the top of my lungs. "You could save him!" I slammed my fists on the steering wheel. "Why won't you do something?! Are you even listening? Where are you, God?!" I needed to hear Him. I need to hear the Creator of the universe tell me everything would be alright.

That's when I heard His quiet still voice, speaking to the depth of my soul, *Sam, I'm right here. I've heard every word and I hold every one of your tears in the palms of My hands. Jordan is My son and I love him, even more than you.*

I opened my eyes, my heart pounding inside my chest.

"This is beyond me, God," I whispered. "This is beyond me." I tried to calm my nerves, shaking inside as His words resonated in my heart. *Jordan is My son and I love him even more than you.*

It was true. Jordan *is* God's son. Ultimately, he doesn't belong to me. I am his earthly father, but Jordan also had a Heavenly Father, and his Heavenly Father loves him far more than I ever could.

But why did God tell me this? Is He asking me to surrender Jordan over to Him? I know I am supposed to trust God no matter what the outcome, but how? How does a parent simply hand over their child? I buried my face in my hands, trying to hold back my tears. "I know you expect this of me, but it's too hard! I can't let go of him."

I thought about the story of Abraham from the Bible. He and his wife Sarah weren't able to have children, yet God promised Abraham his offspring would be as numerous as the stars in Heaven. How could two people in their nineties have children? Logically, it was impossible, but with God everything is possible. God fulfilled His promise through the birth of their son, Isaac. Then years later, God instructed Abraham to kill Isaac as a sacrifice, testing the depth of his faith. I wondered what thoughts ran through

Abraham's mind as he prepared to hand over his son to God? The Bible doesn't share his emotional state, but only reveals Abraham's obedience in doing what God asked. Abraham was expected to love God more than anyone or anything else in the world, including Isaac. And he did. Abraham trusted God would fulfill His promise, whether Isaac lived or died. *Abraham passed the test, but what about me? Could I love God more than Jordan? Would I trust His will over my own?*

It's easier to cling to the things of this world than to cling to God. I was clinging to something that ultimately didn't belong to me. I didn't want Jordan to die, but his fate was out of my control. I used to tell my kids how we are to love God more than anything else, and now I had to live up to my own words. God would have the final say, even if it meant taking Jordan. My faith was standing at a fork in the road and I had to decide which path I would take; trusting God no matter what happens, or not. It was my decision.

"God, help me to love You more than my own family, and accept Your Will no matter what happens. Help me to be all that You need me to be."

That was my prayer, the prayer Jordan said every night before going to sleep. I supposed if I really wanted child-like faith, I needed to start today. I took in several deep breaths, turned on the car, and headed to the hospital. I noticed my phone had several messages from Rosalyn. Not knowing what to expect, I braced myself for the worst.

Chapter Fifteen

When God Speaks

Rosalyn's Story

That morning, the medical team decided to turn off all the machines. Jordan was in and out of a coma, breathing on his own, but the doctors didn't see this as progress and refused any further treatment. I was also told the insurance company wasn't going to cover any more expenses. We were at a dead end with no place to turn. *How did we get to this point?* I thought back to when Jordan first experienced flu like symptoms. *Could I have done anything different? Could the doctors have done anything different?* Only God knew the answer to that question. Jordan's life was slipping through my fingers. My world felt broken and unrepairable. Darkness was closing in and hope was nowhere in sight. I needed to feel God's presence right now. I desperately wanted to hear God's voice, telling me we would somehow survive this.

All I could do was cry as I sat quietly,

looking for any sign of life from Jordan, when one of the doctors appeared at the door with our discharge paperwork.

"Mrs. Allen, I'm Dr. Shire from the ethics committee. I'm very sorry about Jordan, but it just isn't right to prolong his suffering any longer. There's nothing we can do to save your son. If you can't have him transported to another facility by 5:00 pm today, then we'll be forced to take the necessary steps to end his suffering."

"What do you mean by that?" I asked, paralyzed by fear.

"We will turn off the life support machines," Dr. Shire responded calmly.

I studied his face before finally responding. "Dr. Shire, are you a Christian?"

Dr. Shire looked strangely at me, wondering where this was headed.

"Did you pray before making your decision about Jordan? Did God give you the authority to take Jordan's life? Please tell me you at least prayed over this!"

Dr. Shire looked uneasy. His posture shifted as he gazed at the floor. "Mrs. Allen, based on the medical expertise of my team—"

"I don't care about your medical expertise! You made a life and death decision and I want to know if your team prayed over it!"

Dr. Shire looked at Jordan and placed the paperwork on the bed. "I'm very sorry,

Mrs. Allen." He swiftly left the room.

As I watched him disappear down the hospital corridor, I noticed Jordan was still resting, completely oblivious to our conversation. That was a blessing. I sat on his bed, held his hand, and wept.

***

Dr. Shire darted into a restroom. "Did I pray about this?" He mockingly said to himself. "What does prayer have to do with this? I already know all the facts!"

He had thoroughly reviewed Jordan's medical history before making a final decision. Over twenty hours were poured into reading hundreds of medical notes, charts and studying images of Jordan's tumor. Yet, all Mrs. Allen cared about was whether or not he prayed over his decision.

"Nonsense!" Dr. Shire said to himself, discarding any further thought about Jordan's case. As he proceeded to his next meeting, he spotted a statue of Christ prominently displayed in the lobby of the hospital. He walked past it a hundred times a week, but today something prompted him to stop.

"Should I have consulted you?" Dr. Shire asked sarcastically as he stared into the eyes of Jesus. His work environment certainly looked Christian, but what role should faith play in the medical world? He carefully observed others pass by the statue without even a glance. As he continued through the lobby, a particular woman caught his attention. He turned around and watched as she approached the statue, her eyes fixated on Jesus. She stood motionless, bowed her head and prayed as onlookers walked by. He studied her closely, strangely surprised by her public acknowledgment of faith. After a few minutes, she walked towards the elevator and disappeared behind closed metal doors.

Dr. Shire shrugged it off and proceeded to his next meeting, when he caught a glimpse of the hospital's chapel room from the corner of his eye. He stopped and studied the stained-glass window, wondering if anyone on his team had ever stepped inside. He didn't even know if any of them were Christians. The subject of faith never came up in their discussions. For the first time, Dr. Shire decided to open the door and look around. No one was inside.

The outside world was silenced as the door closed behind him. He approached one of the pews and sat quietly. The sunlight poured through the stained glass windows, creating the illusion of a rainbow on the floor leading up to the Alter. Dr. Shire soaked in the tranquility of his surroundings, while just outside the room chaos existed. He noticed a Bible on the pew. For over thirty years, he'd read hundreds of medical journals, yet never once opened a Bible.

What does the Bible have to do with modern medicine? Dr. Shire thought to himself. He'd heard about Jesus curing people miraculously, but that was over two thousand years ago and he didn't believe in modern day miracles.

Dr. Shire noticed a crucifix hanging on the wall. He studied it closely, observing the nails in Jesus' hands and feet. He recalled the Easter story growing up as a child, but so much of what he learned was overshadowed by a large and somewhat-frightening rabbit who delivered candy in a basket. *What's Easter really about? I heard about Jesus coming back to life, but never believed it. How could a man be raised from the dead after spending three days buried in a tomb?* He had a lot of questions about church as a child, but in his household, religion was never discussed. Sadly, he never took the time to explore his faith deeper.

Dr. Shire leaned his head back against the pew, recalling his church memories as a young boy. His father, a successful doctor, attended church every Sunday morning and also made him go. His mother never joined them, claiming she felt poorly. He was nine years old at the time and knew his mother's illness was probably related to her excessive drinking the night before. Often on Sunday morning, he'd wake up before his parents and clean the kitchen counters covered with various liquor bottles, glasses, and filled ashtrays. It was common for his parent's friends to come over Saturday evening and party until the early morning hours. As a child, he would listen from his bedroom to the blaring music and voices singing and laughing all night long. He thought if the kitchen was clean, perhaps his mom might feel better and join them for church, but often this caused more anger from his mother. Her embarrassment stemming from the evening's events overshadowed any level of appreciation.

Despite the late night partying, his dad religiously stuck to his routine, but his brother never went to church. The rule was once you reached high school, church was no longer mandatory. So he and his father sat alone, quietly in the pew and listened to a priest talk about things he never understood. The priest was a tall elderly man with deep wrinkles and a deep voice. His thick-rimmed glasses sat on the edge of his nose as he read from the Bible. Dr. Shire remembered being afraid of how the priest looked at him, for fear his soul had revealed every negative thought he had about being there.

When the organ played its first note, members of the clergy would walk down the aisle, shaking their censers filled with incense. The sanctuary smelled like burned pine bark as he strategically avoided sitting on the end of the pew, trying to distance himself from the smoke.

The most frightening church memory he had was communion. Everyone was summoned to the Alter and drank a horrible tasting wine from the same cup. As a child, his mother ingrained in him the fear of catching germs and was instructed never to share his utensils with anyone. But church required him to break that rule. He recalled numerous times the cup was passed to him from someone who sneezed or was battling an excessive cough. He would spend the rest of the day terrified over getting sick. Nothing irritated his mother more than missing her social luncheons because of a sick kid. He felt like he was being punished for something the church made him do. The only reprieve he had was the glazed donut he received before Sunday school. If he could just survive the forty minute service and communion, a donut would be his reward.

When church was finally over, he and his dad would drive home without any conversation about the service. He had a lot of questions about church and wanted to ask his dad about things written in the Bible. But the one time he brought up the subject, he was reprimanded.

"Never talk about religion, politics, or money. It makes people uncomfortable!" His father replied with a stern voice. So he decided never to ask questions about church again. Besides, in a few years he wouldn't have to go anymore.

As the years passed, he distanced himself from God and poured his time into other things on Sunday morning. Religion never seemed significant to his parents, so why should it be any different for him?

Did you pray before making your decision? Rosalyn's question popped back into his head as his thoughts returned to the present.

"My decisions aren't based on feelings but on facts. Jordan won't live and faith won't change that!" Dr. Shire said out loud, as though speaking to someone in the room.

As he got up abruptly and headed towards the door, a quiet still voice responded. *Jordan will live because faith changes everything.*

He turned around. *Is someone there?* No, he was alone. Yet, the voice seemed real. His attention turned back towards Jesus hanging on the cross. An uneasiness fell upon him, but didn't know why.

Dr. Shire walked towards the Alter and picked up the Bible he saw earlier. Tiny droplets of perspiration glistened on his forehead. He wiped his face with a handkerchief and sat down to catch his breath. Something prompted him to open it. As he read each passage out loud, a voice spoke deep inside. *You call yourself a Christian, but you only know Me by name.*

Dr. Shire looked up. He heard it again, a voice audible only to his heart. *You have no fear of Me. You fear losing your job more than you fear Me.*

Dr. Shire sat motionless, staring at the pages in the Bible. Taking in deep breaths, he read about Jesus' life and how the disciples gave up everything to follow Him. *But why? Why did they risk everything to follow Jesus? Was it because of the miracles He performed? Was He more than just a great teacher?* He paused at the chapter recounting Jesus' suffering. *If He really was the Son of God, why did He die a horrible and tragic death?* Then he got to the part where over five hundred people became witnesses after His resurrection. *Could that many people be delusional at the same time, or did Jesus really rise from the dead?*

Are you aware of all I have given you? Yet, the more I give, the less dependent you become on Me. Do you even know who I Am? Dr. Shire heard the voice again. The more he read, the louder it became.

He placed the Bible back on the pew, pondering what he read. *Could I be wrong about my beliefs? What if everything written in the Bible was actually true? What if eternal life was real? And if it was, where would I be spending mine, Heaven or Hell?* He wanted to believe there was something more, but couldn't fathom believing in an unseen world. Either way, the Bible was very black and white about what was required of the Christian believer. And if you had any doubt, it was best to work it out in this life before it's too late.

His beeper went off. He glanced down and recognized the patient's room number. This family was also facing a life or death decision for their son Daniel Erikson. This child had a brain tumor, but unlike Jordan's, it was operable because of its location. However, the surgery had only a twenty percent chance of survival, and the last time he performed it, his patient went into cardiac arrest and died.

He headed down the hospital corridor and got on the elevator. His mind was racing as he tried to quiet his thoughts and focus on the upcoming surgery. He entered the room of the young boy and noticed his mother sitting by his bedside, praying quietly with her husband. She smiled at him, then he recognized who she was. This was the same woman praying at the statue of Jesus!

The woman looked into his eyes. "Are we ready, Dr. Shire?"

He paused for a moment before answering. He leaned over and held Daniel's hand.

"Yes, we are ready."

Dr. Shire followed behind as the medical team wheeled the young boy into the operating room. He had done this surgery many times before, but sometimes without success. He tried to persuade Daniel's parents not to go through with it, but they refused. He was the hospital's specialist, but Dr. Shire was feeling anxious. *What if Daniel doesn't make it? What if I'm not the expert I think I am?*

"Everything OK, Dr. Shire?" a nurse asked.

"Yes, fine."

Seven hours into the surgery, things seemed to be going smoothly. The tumor was successfully removed. The incision was closed and Dr. Shire took in a deep breath, relieved that everything seemingly went well. At that point, Daniel's blood pressure began to drop.

"What's happening!" Dr. Shire called out. "His pulse is dropping. We're losing him!"

Daniel developed a brain bleed causing cardiac arrest. The medical team frantically tried to stabilize him. Alarms started going off before someone called out, "Code blue!"

This young boy was dying right before his eyes and Dr. Shire didn't know how to stop it. The cardiac team rushed in as Dr.

Shire stepped aside allowing them extra room. His scrubs were soaked in perspiration as he tried to remain calm.

The commotion surrounding him was silenced as he prayed for God to intervene. *Please, not again! Don't let this boy die! I beg you, please.*

What seemed like eternity was only minutes when Dr. Shire finally heard one of the doctors say, "He's gone."

***

Jordan's Story

After finishing my meal with Christopher and Michael, my thoughts returned to my physical condition.

"Everything OK, Jordan?" Michael asked.

"It's my family. They must be so scared over what's happening. If I live, I could tell them everything. I could tell them Heaven is real and warn them about the Devil. But if I die, who will tell them? How will they know?" I said, holding back my tears.

"What makes you think they don't already know?" Michael asked smiling.

"Yeah, but—"

"But what? Then they wouldn't doubt if you told them?" Michael asked. "Come,

Jordan, I want to show you something. Christopher, can I take him for the rest of the day?"

"Of course." Christopher placed his arms around me. "Jordan, your family has a difficult road ahead of them, but Jesus never promised an easy life on earth. What He did promise was to always be with us and would give His strength and peace to sustain us through everything we face."

I hugged Christopher, knowing he was right. Something deep inside told me whatever happened, my family would survive. Michael and I strolled along the pathways amongst the people. I looked towards the Heavenly Mountain in the distance. It was so beautiful, surrounded in light, representing the Glory of God. It was within reach of every person in God's Place of Rest. However, despite its size and beauty, most people still couldn't see it. Their pathways were darkened.

"Jordan, do you see that man over there praying?" Michael asked, nodding in the man's direction.

Peering closely, I noticed it was a doctor. "Do I know him?"

"He knows you. Today, the seed of faith was planted and now we must pray for it to take root."

"Was he an atheist?"

"He claimed to be Christian, yet never

read the Bible. He didn't believe in miracles, yet witnessed them every day. Dr. Shire was one of the most brilliant physicians, but discovered today just how ignorant he truly was."

"What happened?"

"He grew up in a household where faith was supplemental and not fundamental. God was second to everything else, including his work and family. Over time, his soul became deprived as his work became his idol."

"Will he be OK?"

"Only God knows for sure. A radical change has taken place inside of him. But we, as followers of Christ, have to be diligent daily in growing our faith, or we risk losing it altogether. Jesus once said, 'Whoever has will be given more; whoever does not have, even what he has, will be taken from him.'" (Mark 4:25)

"But I thought our salvation was secured."

"Faith can only grow when God becomes the center of your life. That means placing Him above anyone or anything. For many years, Dr. Shire felt being a physician was more important than being a Christian."

"Is that why so many Christians remain unchanged by their faith? Do they think their lives are more important?"

"Jesus once said, 'Apart from me, you

can do nothing.' (John 15:5). Sadly, most people, including Christians, don't believe this. Two people can attend the same church and hear the same sermon, yet only one becomes impacted by the message, while the other remains unchanged."

"How does that happen? How can one person be affected and not the other?"

Michael smiled. "Because one has ears to hear and the other doesn't."

"God must get frustrated to see so many seeds planted that never take root."

"Thankfully, He is a loving and patient God."

As I watched Dr. Shire, I prayed his faith would take root. I prayed he would become divinely changed. I wanted so badly for him to become a Kingdom Child. When you've been changed by faith, you want everyone to experience what you've been given. Before my illness, I never thought much about praying for unbelievers. Now, I prayed for them all the time.

"Jordan, it's time for you to return," Michael said.

I hugged Michael as I thought about everything that's happened.

"Thank you, Michael."

"For what?"

"For protecting me."

"God is your protector," Michael said smiling.

I closed my eyes as Michael prayed over me. In a split second, I returned to the hospital.

***

Dr. Shire's Story

Dr. Shire stood motionless over Daniel, devastated by his death. Feeling lightheaded, he leaned over the hospital bed.

"Dr. Shire, are you alright?" a nurse asked.

He looked at the woman standing next to him; her face covered by a mask; her eyes revealing sorrow and compassion. She gently placed her hand on his arm.

"I need to tell his parents," Dr. Shire said, taking in a deep breath and wiping the tears streaming down his cheeks.

He slipped inside a bathroom to wash his hands and face, thinking about what he would say. As he approached the waiting area, Daniel's parents were in the corner of the room, sitting quietly. His mother was reading a Bible. Dr. Shire watched her closely.

"Mr. and Mrs. Erikson?"

They practically jumped out of their chairs when they heard their name.

"Dr. Shire, how's Daniel?" the woman

asked while holding her husband tightly.

He looked into her eyes.

"Dr. Shire, what happened?" Mr. Erikson asked.

"Daniel didn't—"

"Oh my God! No! Please say it isn't true!" Daniel's mother fell into her husband's arms.

"We did everything we could. I'm so deeply sorry." Dr. Shire gently placed his hand on Mr. Erickson's shoulder.

A nurse approached them and led the couple to a private room. Dr. Shire stood motionless while watching them disappear behind closed doors. He snuck off to his office, wanting to be alone. As he raced through the lobby of the hospital, he stopped at the statue of Jesus.

"I prayed for your help, but you weren't there!"

He slipped inside his office and closed the door. As he stared out the window, he wondered, *At what point did things fall apart? Why did this young boy have to die? Why didn't God answer my prayer?*

His phone rang. The Erikson's wanted to meet with him in the chapel. Dr. Shire looked at his watch. An hour had passed by and no other surgeries were scheduled. He imagined the ethics committee was gathering to discuss the death of Daniel Erickson. It was just a matter of time before his day would be filled with meetings reviewing every detail of the surgery. Dr. Shire headed to the chapel, his mind spinning. He slowly opened the door and saw the couple sitting quietly on the front pew looking at a crucifix.

"Mr. and Mrs. Erikson?" Dr. Shire walked up slowly and sat next to them. No one spoke for what seemed like eternity.

"Dr. Shire," Daniel's mother started, "we just wanted to thank you for all you've done. We knew this surgery was risky, and even if Daniel lived, there may have been complications."

Dr. Shire sat quietly, trying to process everything. "I'm so sorry, Mrs. Erickson. We all had high hopes Daniel would get through this. I'm devastated as well," he said, sniffling, holding back his tears.

"It wasn't God's plan," Mr. Erickson spoke softly.

"God's plan?" Dr. Shire asked.

Mr. Erikson looked curiously. "Do you not believe in the sovereignty of God?"

Dr. Shire was speechless.

"Dr. Shire, everything that happens is about furthering God's kingdom, even suffering to the point of death. Do you believe that?"

"I don't know what to believe," Dr. Shire confessed, shaking his head. "It's hard to believe in God when something like this happens."

The couple sat their quietly, looking down at the floor.

Finally Daniel's mother spoke. "It's harder not to believe in God when something like this happens. Perhaps one day you will understand what that means." She stood and hugged Dr. Shire before she and her husband left the chapel.

Dr. Shire was alone, tears welled in his eyes. He thought about their conversation, and despite the tragic set of circumstances, Daniel's parents somehow had an inner peace about them.

It wasn't God's plan for Daniel to survive? He asked himself. *How could anything good come from this?* Dr. Shire didn't know. But as he stared at a Bible placed next to him, he wondered if the answers might be found inside.

Chapter Sixteen

Saving Faith

Rosalyn's Story

When Sam arrived, I told him the hospital's decision to end Jordan's life. Sam immediately got on the phone with a local television station and shared our story. The station aired it, and within a few hours, our prayers were answered. The director of a medical facility contacted us and said Jordan could stay there as long as needed. We were overjoyed by the news and had him transported immediately.

After several months at this facility, Jordan's condition remained unchanged and we decided to bring him home. Although he was still in a coma, Christmas was around the corner and our family didn't want to celebrate it in a hospital. Jordan had a feeding tube, but for the most part, he was breathing on his own. At times, Jordan seemed to want to keep on fighting for his life. The way he looked at me provided hope that God might heal him.

But other times, his eyes would open slightly, revealing a soul trapped inside his body, wanting to be free from disease. I was conflicted on what we should do. We needed God to have the final say over Jordan's life.

***

Jordan's Story

I could faintly hear my family's voices around me. At times, my mind was alert, although I could barely open my eyes. I felt Paige sitting next to me in my bed as she watched TV. She would talk to me and constantly kiss my hand. The old me would have been annoyed, but the new me loved having her near. Paige and Bear were not only family, they were my best friends.

Most people stopped coming by because it was hard for them to see me like this, but Paige had the gift of seeing beyond my illness. In her mind, I was taking a long nap and would soon wake up.

One evening while Paige was helping with dinner, I heard a strange deep voice by my bedside. I knew immediately it was the Devil.

"Jordan, what kind of God would do this to you and your family? How could a God of love allow all this suffering? Why won't He heal you? Worship me and I will heal you." His voice sounded like a drum beating on the bedroom walls.

My heart cried out, "In the name of Jesus, get out!" The devil left abruptly. Strangely, my family didn't hear a thing as they continued talking in the kitchen.

"Jordan."

This time it was Christopher's voice in my room. Feeling relieved, my spirit smiled.

"I could use some help in the vineyard. Are you up for it?"

I raised my hand and in a split second, we were standing in God's Place of Rest.

***

Rosalyn's Story

After several weeks, I noticed Jordan was having difficulty breathing. Every few minutes, we administered breathing treatments to help air flow into his lungs. Pneumonia was also a concern, but none of his doctors were willing to treat him anymore.

One rainy morning, Jordan's nurse and I worked diligently giving him breathing treatments and suctioning his nose. I was afraid his lungs were filling with fluid. Jordan seemed peaceful, but I was becoming more anxious. Sam and I had been up all night worried he might stop breathing altogether. I called two of my friends to come over in the morning and pray, hoping God would intervene.

There was still a part of me who believed Jordan would be healed miraculously, but there was another part of me who tried to prepare for the worst. At times, it felt like I was floating on a raft in the middle of the ocean, waiting to be rescued by God. It would have been easier to slip off the raft and plunge into a deep dark abyss, but I couldn't go there. I had to hold on.

***

Jordan's Story

As we walked towards the vineyard, I noticed several workers tilling the soil and watering each vine. So much care and detail went into each plant. As we walked down a row, I noticed a particular vine with a bunch of grapes.

"Wow! That's a really healthy one. I bet some really good wine will come from that."

Christopher smiled. "Yes, and I have you to thank for that."

"But I'm only aware of a few people who were changed by my situation."

"Let me show you something." Christopher took me to an unfamiliar place.

"Where are we?"

"Africa," Christopher replied. "Look over there."

To my surprise I saw Dr. Canon in the distance treating several sick children.

"Dr. Canon was transformed by faith, and each year he spends several months here providing medical assistance. Your condition played a big part in leading him to the right path.

"Wow! That's really cool! Do those grapes represent some of the children?"

"Yes, they do. Remember, you can only see a ripple of what your faith has done for others."

We stood and watched Dr. Canon for quite some time.

"If I live, I want to be a doctor and help others in Africa."

"You will live and have already helped many in Africa," Christopher responded.

As we walked along, we came to a river bank and sat for a moment. There was a basket of fresh fruit and warm baked bread waiting for us. Christopher broke the bread and prayed. While enjoying our meal, I noticed a band of angels standing on the other side of the river bank. They circled around the wandering people.

"What are they doing?"

"They're waiting to be called into battle."

Just then a black mass resembling a dark storm cloud appeared overhead, looming over many of the lost souls, but they couldn't see it.

"What's going on?" I asked, feeling anxious.

"Those are demons hovering over the people," Christopher responded.

"Why don't the angels go after them?"

"Because the angels are waiting for God's command, and God is waiting for the people to ask for His help."

"Don't they see the darkness?" I pointed at the demons in astonishment.

"No, and even worse, their unbelief leaves them unarmed for battle."

As the darkness got closer, I realized the cloud was actually a giant swarm of flies. At once, the flies changed into demons of all sizes laughing and clawing at the people.

"Oh my gosh!" I stood and watched in disbelief. People were crying and screaming, but no one was calling out to Jesus. "If they only believed, Jesus would rescue them right?"

"Of course, He would."

I felt a deep pain in my heart, witnessing so many people entrapped by the spiritual warfare going on around them. So many of the wandering souls cried out in anguish. But the more they cried, the louder the demons taunted them. All you could hear were lies spewing from the demon's mouths, "No one can help you! You're not worth anything! Go ahead and kill yourself. God could never love you!"

I stood there, watching the souls become filled with despair until I couldn't take it any longer. I tore down the mountain hoping to rescue at least one more life from the darkness. I turned around and saw Christopher was following behind.

"Leave her alone! In the name Jesus, get away from her!" I screamed at a demon tormenting a young woman. It screamed vile obscenities at me, while the woman stared in confusion.

"Who are you? Why are yelling at me?" she cried out.

"I'm not yelling at you," I responded. "I'm yelling at the demon to get away from you."

"What are you saying?" She asked, backing away as though I was the fearful one.

"If you would turn your life over to Christ, this darkness would leave. Just believe!"

"Jesus? Oh yes, the Son of God," she replied sarcastically. "Why do you believe in such fairy tales? If there was a God, why would He allow horrible things to happen?"

As she said this, I heard a man screaming in the distance. A demon was torturing him. I ran over to see if I could help.

"In the name of Jesus, get away from him!" I screamed.

The demon stepped away and watched while the man looked at me curiously.

"If you would give your life to Christ, you could overcome this pain! I promise. Just listen to me!"

The man looked into my eyes with such sadness and helplessness. "I believed once in Jesus," he said, "but I can't believe again. He wanted too much of me." The man turned and walked away.

I was shocked by his statement, believing all hope was lost. I fell to the ground and cried.

"Christopher, what do we do? Can't we help them?"

He picked me up from the ground. "Your faith can help them. Just believe and pray for them. Intercessory prayer is very powerful."

"What is intercessory prayer?"

"God hears all prayers, but the prayers from His Kingdom Children are meaningful. Because of your faith, perhaps one of the souls you encounter will be healed."

I closed my eyes and looked up to the sky, feeling the warmth of the light on my cheeks as it rained down from the sky. "Oh

Jesus, please help me to help others. Help these people to believe in you. If only they could see you, then perhaps they'd believe."

When I opened my eyes, I noticed Christopher was no longer Christopher. Every pore in his body glistened with beautiful radiant light. I stared in amazement as he transformed right before my eyes. "Oh my gosh! What in the world? You're not Christopher. You're... you're Jesus!"

Jesus smiled as He held me close.

"I didn't know Christopher was You," I said, turning around to see if any of the people recognized Jesus standing before them.

"They can't see you!" I cried out.

"No, they can't, yet I manifest myself every day to God's children."

I stood in disbelief while watching others walk right past us. However, the demons recognized Jesus and immediately ran away screaming.

"Will they ever see You?"

Jesus looked into the eyes of the wandering people as though He was looking into their souls. His expression revealed the depth of His love for each individual. He knew their pains and their joys. He knew their troubles and their choices they'd made. Jesus walked through the masses waiting to hear His name, but no one cried out His name. Yet He stood patiently, waiting and watching.

"It is only by faith that they can see Me. They must believe."

Frustration boiled up inside of me as I grabbed one of the standstills.

"Jesus is right here. Can't you see Him! Can't you believe!"

The standstill looked blankly at me. "I don't need God's help. I've always lived my life just fine without anyone's help."

I ran up to another soul, a woman crying along the pathway.

"Jesus loves you and wants to help you. All you have to do is pray to Him and believe."

But she looked at me blankly. "I believed once, but my prayers were never answered. I can't believe again."

My heart fell as I wept for these people.

Jesus took my hand and sat me on a rock, holding me close.

"Jordan, I will not force Myself upon anyone," Jesus said. "Faith is a personal choice. Nobody's destiny is made for them. We choose our own pathways."

"I just don't understand why so many reject you?" But as I looked at the people wandering along, so many had.

"Many can't see themselves for who or what they really are. They think in their nicety, they will make it to Heaven, but even the nicest people can spend eternity in Hell.

The human heart cannot love God or ever please Him. One must be born again. One must become a Kingdom Child and that only happens to those whom the Father draws to Me."

The darkness continued to hover at a distance while God's angels waited for His command, but nothing happened. No one was praying. No one wanted God's help.

"So, it's hopeless?"

"Where there's breath, there's hope," Jesus said, holding me close.

"What can I do Jesus? How do I reach these people? I'll do anything to try to save them!" As I buried my face into His side, I recalled the time with Sarah seeing firsthand the lake of fire. So many tormented lives filled with pain and agony would remain there for all eternity. The thought of it made me sick.

Jesus sat quietly, still waiting on the people. He looked up into the sky and began to pray, but I couldn't understand what He was saying. When Jesus finished, He looked into my eyes. "There is one thing you can do, Jordan."

"What is it?"

"Are you willing to die for Me so that others might live?" He asked.

For a moment, I couldn't speak. That was the ultimate question. Every Christian must be willing to be all that Christ calls them to be, even if it leads to death.

My entire journey flashed before my eyes beginning with my initial prayer. That simple prayer of asking God to help me be all that He wanted me to be led me down a pathway of suffering even to the point of death. Yet along the way, my life was transformed. I not only witnessed miracles, I was a miracle! Physically, I was dying, but spiritually I was made new. I experienced the power of the Holy Spirit through spiritual warfare. I saw angels and demons. I could look inside the souls of human beings. And through it all, I became a Kingdom Child. I had accomplished more in fourteen years than many of these people would ever accomplish. There was nothing more important than knowing my name was written in the Book of Life.

I studied the people wandering along the pathways. How many of them were murderers? How many of them were atheists? How many claimed to be Christian but had lukewarm faith? How many believed what they said they believed? All of humanity was right before my eyes, and sadly many didn't recognize Jesus sitting right in front of them. In order to know God, they had to know His Son. There was no other way into Heaven.

It felt like a million eyes were on me as the angels waited for my response. Michael appeared in the crowd looking just like he did the first day we met: long white hair, crystal-blue eyes, wearing a denim shirt and jeans. His expression was filled with love and compassion as he looked into my eyes. I smiled at him while reaching inside my pocket, searching for any remaining seeds, but it was empty.

"I'm out of seeds." I said looking blankly at Jesus.

"That's because you've finished the race. You became all that I needed you to be," Jesus said smiling. "And I'm giving you the crown of life."

To hear those words brought such joy to my heart. All along, the only thing I had to do was believe and trust God no matter what the outcome. At times, cancer seemed bigger than God and the thought of death left me so afraid, but because of my faith, everything changed. I wasn't afraid of cancer and I certainly wasn't afraid to die. Jesus is real, Heaven is real, and death would never be my destiny.

"I would gladly die for you, Jesus," I said smiling.

Jesus beamed as the angels shouted with joy.

"Before I go, can I do one thing?"

"What's that?" Jesus replied.

"May I tell Mom how much I love her and my family?"

"Yes, that would be a wonderful thing

to do." Jesus took my hand and led me to the top of the Heavenly Mountain. The gates of Heaven opened up as I looked into the eyes of the people smiling and waving me in. It was the most amazing experience of my life. I can't explain the joy you have when you enter Heaven. It was even more beautiful than God's Place of Rest. These people had no sorrow, no pain, and no disease. In fact, they looked more alive than most human beings I knew on earth. And the best thing about it was I would never battle Satan again. As I walked with Jesus, I became overwhelmed with joy and the freedom of leaving my physical body once and for all. As each person greeted me, I noticed them holding a puzzle piece in their hand.

"Why do they each have a puzzle piece?"

But before He could answer, Sarah appeared out of the crowd and ran over to hug me and Jesus. She was so excited to see me. "Jordan, you're here! Thank you for all that you did for my dad! He's saved! Now I know he'll be OK. Do you have your puzzle piece?"

I looked at her strangely while digging deep inside my pocket. To my surprise, I pulled out a piece. She took it from me and it fit perfectly with hers.

"How did that happen?"

"All of our pieces fit together because every child belonging to God becomes connected through Christ," Sarah replied. "On the last day, all of the pieces from every Kingdom Child will be gathered and we will see how our lives became connected through faith."

"That will be one amazing puzzle!" I exclaimed.

Sarah laughed while we walked down the golden streets. The best way to describe Heaven is one word: paradise.

Jesus showed me the place He had prepared for my family. My grandmother was waiting for me with open arms. We talked for quite some time while enjoying a meal with Jesus and Sarah. I couldn't wait for the rest of my family to join us one day.

"Come, Jordan," Jesus said. "There's work to be done, even in Heaven. The harvest is plentiful and the workers are few."

"I'm ready." Heaven was home and I still had work to do for those left behind. As I looked upon God's Place of Rest from Heaven, I noticed Michael in the midst of the wandering souls. He looked up at me and waved.

"He never stops working, does he, Jesus?" I asked, waving to him from the mountain.

"No, he never does. He is on his way to protect others who call on My name."

I hoped one day Michael would protect Paige. He was the coolest angel of all.

***

Rosalyn's Story

My two friends arrived and prayed while the nurse and I struggled with Jordan's breathing. He was really laboring and I didn't know how much more he could endure. It was a rainy Monday morning and I tried to stay calm. I looked up and noticed Jordan's eyes were wide open. He was looking at me and his lips were moving as though he was trying to say something.

"Jordan! Baby, you're awake!" I screamed out.

For a moment, Jordan's eyes were open. I hadn't seen the white of his eyes for months and now my son was looking at me. His expression was filled with love as I watched his tender lips move. Jordan was trying to tell me something.

"What do you want to say, sweetie?"

He looked deeply into my eyes, but I couldn't understand what he was saying. For a moment, it felt like it was just Jordan and me in the room alone, having a conversation. Noise and confusion were all around us, yet I remained focused on him, hoping God would give me the ultimate miracle.

The nurse grabbed the phone and

called 911. Within minutes, firemen were pounding on the front door. One of my friends ran to let them in and they raced into the room, lifted Jordan out of my arms and placed him on the floor. *Was Jordan dying? No, that couldn't be happening. He was conscious and awake. His lips were moving.* The fear in the paramedic's eyes was overwhelming. I had just seen a miracle, but he was looking at something totally different.

They tried to resuscitate Jordan before placing him on a stretcher. They raced out the door with my baby boy and put him in the ambulance. I got in my friend's car and we followed the ambulance to the hospital. Neither one of us spoke in the car as we were trying to process what happened. She dropped me off and left to park the car. I called Sam while running through the building screaming for my son. A nurse led me to a room where doctors were desperately trying to get a heartbeat out of my precious boy.

"Come on, baby, come back!" I cried out. Everything was falling apart right before my eyes.

The room became quiet.

One of the doctor's turned to look at me, his eyes filled with sorrow. "I'm sorry. We did everything we could. He's gone."

"No! No! Please save him!" I cried out as I ran over to Jordan's bedside. I held him in my arms, hoping once more God would bring

him back. But this time, God didn't. My baby
was gone.

Chapter Seventeen

Where Do We Go From Here

Rosalyn's Story

Today our family is minus one. I don't know why God allowed us only fourteen years with Jordan. I'll never understand everything that happened. But this I do know: God loved Jordan more than I ever could, and I know for certain Jordan is in Heaven.

Every day I think about him and the laughter he brought to our family. Jordan was wise beyond his years. Often when he spoke, it was like listening to a wise old man trapped inside a child's body. He was very mature for his age. Most kids have a self-centered life, placing their needs before anyone else's. Jordan was different. His needs were always second to others.

Every Friday night after work, our family gathered at my mom's house for dinner. For years, this was a family tradition. However, one Friday fell on my birthday and I didn't feel like celebrating with everyone. I preferred a quiet evening at home with my family. When Jordan found out, I'll never forget what he said. "Mama, you can celebrate your birthday any day of the week, but tonight we're going to Grandma's." He intuitively knew how upset my mom would be and made sure we didn't sway from our family commitments.

As I look back, I must admit I wish things had been different. I never thought in a million years I would lose my child. Through it all, I held on to the hope that Jordan might live and I never gave up until he took his last breath. In our final moments together, I got to see my son look right into my eyes. His lips were moving and I believe he was trying to tell me something. Perhaps he wanted me to know how much he loved all of us.

My faith in God and in the resurrection is what I lean on for survival. I could spend the rest of my days asking God, 'Why me?' 'Why my family?' But truthfully, the real question I should ask is, 'Why not me?' We live in a broken fallen world and Jordan was blessed to go early. I have peace knowing he truly is in a better place. God can do wonderful things, even in our most tragic moments. My prayer today is for God to use our loss to bring others to Christ. So many say they believe, but their actions reflect differently. I pray I never become like that. I pray I can be there for Paige, and that through this she will become stronger in her faith. It's only by God's grace and His strength that I can survive this loss. And some day, this complicated puzzle piece that was handed to me will make perfect sense.

***

Sam's Story

My life will never be the same without Jordan. There is a void in my heart that I know only God can fill. When a child dies, it goes outside the bounds of what we consider to be the natural order of life. Children live and old people die. That's how humans think, but that's not always how God thinks. God's ways are beyond our ways.

I can't believe Jordan is gone. I think about going to football games, but stop myself the moment I realize I would be going without my son. I come home from work thinking I'll walk in Jordan's room and he'll be there, then realize Jordan will never be there again. I am still at a loss and shaken by the events of what happened. But through it all, I have been given the gift of peace to face each day knowing that God had the final say over Jordan's life.

If there's one thing I've learned, Jordan was never mine. He always belonged

to God. I had received the gift of a son to
raise, nurture, love, and enjoy for fourteen
wonderful years. We can't hold on to the
things of this world too tightly because
nothing is in our control. The more I come to
accept that, the easier Jordan's death
becomes. Jordan's life has made me a better
person, a better father and husband. Most
importantly, my life was transformed by faith.
It would be easier to be mad at God for taking
Jordan, but I refuse to go there. If you truly
believe in the Christian faith, then everything
we have ultimately belongs to God. And I am
thankful that Jordan's death has placed me on
the pathway to everlasting life.

I hope others who read our story will
find peace knowing there's a death that leads
to life and a life that leads to death. It's never
about being the best we can be. It's about
being all God calls us to be. That's the
ultimate question; are we all that God calls us
to be? Jordan is a Kingdom Child, and I, too,
can now claim this title.

***

Paige's Story

Jordan wasn't supposed to die. I never
believed he would. I thought for sure God
would save him. But Mom tells me God's

ways are not always our ways. My life is different without Jordan…will never be the same. But this I do know: Jordan is in Heaven and he would have wanted it to be this way. He always said he was glad God didn't allow this to happen to my life. Someday, we'll see each other again. Until then, I have to figure out how not to miss him so much. Jordan was always around. It's strange not to see him in his room or downstairs watching TV. I still look for him as though he's going to appear around the corner, waiting to walk me home from school. My parents talk about him all the time, which helps. I like to talk about Jordan because when I do, it makes me think of all the happy times we had together. His presence is still very real to me, even though I know he's with God. Yet, a part of him will always be with me. I can still hear his voice crystal clear as though he is standing right next to me. Heaven isn't far away. Jordan is still within reach of holding my hand.

***

Bear's Story

Jordan's death seems like yesterday. I can still hear his voice calling out to me to play football or tag with Paige. Although I was many years older than Jordan, he was many years wiser than me. He had a connection with God that I hope to have one day. I'll never forget the day he and Paige were baptized. He was paralyzed in a wheel chair, yet was determine to be dunked in water for an entire congregation to witness.

So where do I stand in all of this? Jordan's death has caused me to look deeply at my own faith. Jordan was the image of someone whose death led others to become Christ followers. Some day God will explain this to me, but today I hope to have the kind of faith that Jordan had.

Chapter Eighteen

God Will Have the Final Say

1 In the beginning was the Word, and the Word was with God, and the Word was God. [2] He was with God in the beginning. [3] Through Him all things were made; without Him nothing was made that has been made.[4] In Him was life, and that life was the light of all mankind. [5] The light shines in the darkness, and the darkness has not overcome[a] it. (John 1: 1-5)

10 He was in the world, and though the world was made through Him, the world did not recognize Him. (John 1:10)

Jesus is the light and the life. God's desire for mankind is to be in relationship through His Son and to live for His plan and His purpose.

27So God created mankind in His own image, in the image of God He created them;

male and female He created them. (Genesis 1:27)

13 For you created my inmost being; you knit me together in my mother's womb.

(Psalm 139:13)

16 Your eyes saw my unformed body; all the days ordained for me were written in Your book before one of them came to be. (Psalm 139:16)

However, when sin entered the world, everything changed.

19 By the sweat of your brow you will eat your food until you return to the ground, since from it you were taken; for dust you are and to dust you will return." (Genesis 3:19)

Man no longer lived to please God, but instead lived to please himself. God allows free will and the choice is ours whether or not to obey Him. However, the decision we make reveals the pathway we're on; life or death.

5Surely I was sinful at birth, sinful from the time my mother conceived me. (Psalm 51:5)

18 For I know that good itself does not dwell in me, that is, in my sinful nature. [a] For I have the desire to do what is good, but I cannot carry it out. (Romans 7:18)

Because of our sinful nature, we are naturally inclined to rebel against God.

23But I see another law at work in me, waging war against the law of my mind and making me a prisoner of the law of sin at work within me. (Romans 7:23)

By living to please our sinful nature, our pathway leads to death. However, when we choose to live according to the Spirit, our lives are changed forever and we are placed on the pathway that leads to eternal life.

6 Jesus answered, "I am the way and the truth and the life. No one comes to the Father except through Me." (John 14:6)

The Bible states there's only one way to Heaven and that's through Jesus. It is His deepest desire for us to live with Him in the kingdom of Heaven.

3The Lord is not slow in keeping His promise, as some understand slowness. Instead, He is patient with you, not wanting anyone to perish, but everyone to come to repentance. (2Peter 3:9)

He is in constant pursuit of our heart in hopes that we will choose the pathway of repentance, turning from old ways and striving to become more like Him.

As we live out our days, every decision we make impacts the pathway we're on. Our actions speak louder than our words. Even Christians stray from the pathway to Heaven.

4It is impossible for those who have once been enlightened, who have tasted the heavenly gift, who have shared in the Holy Spirit, 5 who have tasted the goodness of the Word of God and the powers of the coming age 6 and who have fallen[a] away, to be brought back to repentance. To their loss they are crucifying the Son of God all over again and subjecting Him to public disgrace. (Hebrews 6:4-6)

As we live out our days, the Creator of the Universe may only be a passing thought, if even a thought at all. Perhaps the seed of faith was planted, but it never took root. As a result, one's faith is tossed like waves blown by the wind. And when trials come unexpectedly, we begin to doubt.

10 Do not be afraid of what you are about to suffer. I tell you, the Devil will put some of you in prison to test you, and you will suffer persecution for ten days. Be faithful, even to the point of death, and I will give you life as your victor's crown. (Revelation 2:10)

Sexual immorality, idolatry, and worshiping other gods also take us down the pathway of destruction. When we choose our own personal desires over what God desires for us, we fall away from God.

1 You have searched me, Lord, and You know me. (Psalm 139:1)

23 Search me, God, and know my heart; test me and know my anxious thoughts. (Psalm 139:23)

We can't hide from God. He knows our every thought, word, and deed. He knows every moment of joy, pain, and suffering in our lives. And by His grace, He forgives us for our sins, even though we rebel.

9 The Lord our God is merciful and forgiving, even though we have rebelled against Him; (Daniel 9:9)

10 "But I want you to know that the Son of Man has authority on earth to forgive sins."
(Mark 2:10)

28 Truly, I tell you, people can be forgiven all their sins and every slander they utter,
(Mark 3:28)

Many claim to know Jesus, but by the way they live their lives, they only know Him by name. Sadly, many believers think they're on the pathway to life when actually they're headed for destruction.

5 Jesus answered, "Very truly I tell you, no one can enter the kingdom of God unless they are born of water and the Spirit."
(John 3:5)

21 "Not everyone who says to me, 'Lord, Lord,' will enter the kingdom of heaven, but only the one who does the will of My Father who is in heaven. 22 Many will say to Me on that day, 'Lord, Lord, did we not prophesy in Your name and in Your name drive out demons, and in Your name perform many miracles?' 23 Then I will tell them plainly, 'I never knew you. Away from me, you evildoers!'" (Matthew 7:21-23)

Faith is more than a weekly church service. It's more than doing good deeds and being a nice person. Faith is a gift and is given to those who seek Christ fully.

7 "Ask and it will be given to you; seek and you will find; knock and the door will be opened to you." (Matthew 7:7)

Seek God in everything. Otherwise, we risk becoming complacent, causing our faith to become lukewarm.

11 We want each of you to show this same diligence to the very end, so that what you hope for may be fully realized. 12 We do not want you to become lazy, but to imitate those who through faith and patience inherit what has been promised. (Hebrews 6:11-12)

16 "So, because you are lukewarm—neither hot nor cold—I am about to spit you out of my mouth." (Revelation 3:16)

We must believe and never doubt and strive to be all who Christ calls us to be, even when it goes against the world's standards. Do we care more about what the world thinks of us than what God thinks? Sadly, at times, we do. Social media has become our "god" as we spend endless hours consumed by technology, leading us more and more into confusion, and creating division amongst our family and friends.

17 From the rest he makes a god, his idol; he bows down to it and worships. He prays to it and says, "Save me! You are my god!" (Isaiah 44:17)

Satan has deceived us by creating an illusion over where our priorities ought to be. For example: Do we spend more time studying our 401K's than we do studying God's Word?

17 You may say to yourself, "My power and the strength of my hands have produced this wealth for me." 18 But remember the Lord your God, for it is He who gives you the ability to produce wealth, and so confirms His covenant, which He swore to your ancestors, as it is today. (Deuteronomy 8:17-18)

17 You say, 'I am rich; I have acquired wealth and do not need a thing.' But you do not realize that you are wretched, pitiful, poor, blind, and naked. (Revelation 3:17)

Place your trust in God instead of the world, and all you need will be provided.

17 Command those who are rich in this present world not to be arrogant nor to put their hope in wealth, which is so uncertain, but to put their hope in God, Who richly provides us with everything for our enjoyment. (1Timothy 6:17)

25 "Therefore I tell you, do not worry about your life, what you will eat or drink; or about your body, what you will wear. Is not life more than food, and the body more than clothes?

26 Look at the birds of the air; they do not sow or reap or store away in barns, and yet your

Heavenly Father feeds them. Are you not much more valuable than they? 27 Can any one of you by worrying add a single hour to your life[a]? 28 "And why do you worry about clothes? See how the flowers of the field grow. They do not labor or spin. 29 Yet I tell you that not even Solomon in all his splendor was dressed like one of these. 30 If that is how God clothes the grass of the field, which is here today and tomorrow is thrown into the fire, will He not much more clothe you—you of little faith? 31 So do not worry, saying, 'What shall we eat?' or 'What shall we drink?' or 'What shall we wear?' 32 For the pagans run after all these things, and your Heavenly Father knows that you need them. 33 But seek first His kingdom and His righteousness, and all these things will be given to you as well. 34 Therefore, do not worry about tomorrow, for tomorrow will worry about itself. Each day has enough trouble of its own." (Matthew 6:25-34)

So how we do seek His Kingdom first? It begins by trusting God and obeying His Word. It means to live out our faith seven days a week, 24 hours a day.

22 Do not merely listen to the Word, and so deceive yourselves. Do what it says.

23 Anyone who listens to the Word but does not do what it says is like someone who looks at his face in a mirror 24 and, after looking at himself, goes away and

immediately forgets what he looks like. 25 But whoever looks intently into the perfect law that gives freedom and continues in it—not forgetting what they have heard but doing it—they will be blessed in what they do. (James 1:22-25)

Leaders of the church have a divine calling, and this task should never be taken lightly. But even the most educated theologians wander off the pathway of life when they begin to spread false teaching.

11 They must be silenced, because they are disrupting whole households by teaching things they ought not to teach—and that for the sake of dishonest gain. (Titus 1:11)

8 But you have turned from the way and by your teaching have caused many to stumble; you have violated the covenant with Levi," says the Lord Almighty. (Malachi 2:8)

3 For the time will come when people will not put up with sound doctrine. Instead, to suit their own desires, they will gather around them a great number of teachers to say what their itching ears want to hear. 4 They will turn their ears away from the truth and turn aside to myths. (2Timothy 4:3-4)

Sermons shouldn't be about what we want to hear, but what we need to hear. How often do churches preach about Hell? How often are congregations warned about Satan and his dominion? Jesus talked a lot about Heaven, but He also talked a lot about Satan and Hell. Christians have no reason to fear Satan; however, his existence shouldn't be ignored.

12 "Therefore rejoice you heavens and you who dwell in them! But woe to the earth and the sea, because the Devil has gone down to you! He is filled with fury, because he knows that his time is short." (Revelation 12:12)

18 He replied, "I saw Satan fall like lightning from heaven. (Luke 10:18-19)

Satan is a real spiritual being and not just an embodiment of evil. He has been allowed to live amongst us on earth for a period of time and has one and only one mission: to destroy lives! However, we needn't fear Satan since God has empowered the Christian believer with His arsenal to face any spiritual battle that we may face.

10 Finally, be strong in the Lord and in His mighty power. 11 Put on the full armor of God, so that you can take your stand against the Devil's schemes. 12 For our struggle is not against flesh and blood, but against the rulers, against the authorities, against the powers of this dark world, and against the spiritual forces of evil in the heavenly realms. 13 Therefore, put on the full armor of God, so that when the day of evil comes, you may be able to stand your ground, and after you have done everything, to stand. 14 Stand firm then, with the belt of truth buckled around your

waist, with the breastplate of righteousness in place, 15 and with your feet fitted with the readiness that comes from the gospel of peace. 16 In addition to all this, take up the shield of faith, with which you can extinguish all the flaming arrows of the evil one. 17 Take the helmet of salvation and the sword of the Spirit, which is the word of God. (Ephesians 6:10-17)

The only thing Christians need to fear is God. Be reverent in worship and honor Him in everything.

13 To fear the Lord is to hate evil: I hate pride and arrogance, evil behavior and perverse speech. (Proverbs 8:13)

13 Yet because the wicked do not fear God, it will not go well with them, and their days will not lengthen like a shadow. (Ecclesiastes 8:13)

So often the trials in life point us down a different pathway, especially when outcomes weren't what we hoped for. God has a lot to say about suffering and often it's our suffering that brings us closer to Him.

12 Blessed is the one who perseveres under trial because, having stood the test, that person will receive the crown of life that the Lord has promised to those who love Him. (James 1:12)

No one will have an excuse for not knowing God.

18 The wrath of God is being revealed from heaven against all the godlessness and wickedness of people, who suppress the truth by their wickedness, 19 since what may be known about God is plain to them, because God has made it plain to them. 20 For since the creation of the world, God's invisible qualities—his eternal power and divine nature—have been clearly seen, being understood from what has been made, so that people are without excuse. (Romans1:18-20)

21 For although they knew God, they neither glorified Him as God nor gave thanks to Him, but their thinking became futile and their foolish hearts were darkened. (Romans 1:21)

The time is now to be all God calls us to be so that our lives can be a reflection of Christ. We are living in end times and many are unprepared for Christ's return.

7 Nation will rise against nation, and kingdom against kingdom. There will be famines and earthquakes in various places. 8 All these are the beginning of birth pains. (Matthew 24:7-8)

"Many fall away from the faith. Hatred and wickedness will grow in people's hearts.

12 Because of the increase of wickedness, the love of most will grow cold (Matthew 24:12)

Therefore, as a Kingdom Child, pray for unbelievers and remain united in Christ. It is the highest calling we have on this earth and one that should never be taken lightly. Be strong in the Lord and in His mighty power! God will never abandon us nor forsake us.

6 Be strong and courageous. Do not be afraid or terrified because of them, for the Lord your God goes with you; He will never leave you nor forsake you. (Deuteronomy 31:6)

13 "Enter through the narrow gate. For wide is the gate and broad is the road that leads to destruction, and many enter through it. 14 But small is the gate and narrow the road that leads to life, and only a few find it. (Matthew 7:13-14)

19 Therefore go and make disciples of all nations, baptizing them in the name of the Father and of the Son and of the Holy Spirit, 20 and teaching them to obey everything I have commanded you. And surely, I am with you always, to the very end of the age." (Matthew 28:19-20)

Never forget how much God loves us. His one and only Son died on our behalf so that we could live with Him forever!

16 For God so loved the world that He gave His one and only Son, that whoever believes in Him shall not perish but have eternal life. (John 3:16)

12 "Look, I am coming soon! My reward is with Me, and I will give to each person according to what they have done. 13 I am the Alpha and the Omega, the First and the Last, the Beginning and the End. (Revelation 22:12-13)

The End

Jordan Allen

Paige, Rosalyn, Sam and Bear Allen

Jennifer Johnson and Rosalyn Allen

~*~*~*~